SPEAK UP!

Stephanie Perry Moore

SPEAK UP!

Morgan Love Series
Book 2

MOODY PUBLISHERS
CHICAGO

All Scripture quotations are taken from the *New American Standard Bible®*, Copyright © 1960, 1962, 1963, 1968, 1971, 1972, 1973, 1975, 1977, 1995 by the Lockman Foundation. Used by permission. (www.Lockman.org)

Edited by Kathryn Hall
Interior design: Ragont Design
Cover design and image: TS Design Studio
Author photo: Bonnie Rebholz
Word searches by Pam Pugh

Some definitions found at the end of chapters are from WordSmyth.net.

Library of Congress Cataloging-in-Publication Data

Moore, Stephanie Perry.
    Speak up! / Stephanie Perry Moore.
        p. cm. -- (Morgan Love series ; #2)
    Summary: Seven-year-old Morgan asks Jesus for guidance when her friend Trey starts hanging around the class bully. Educational exercises provided at the end of each chapter.
    ISBN 978-0-8024-2264-4
    [1. Bullies—Fiction. 2. Schools—Fiction. 3. Conduct of life—Fiction. 4. Christian life—Fiction. 5. African Americans—Fiction.]
    I. Title.
PZ7.M788125Sp 2011
[Fic]—dc22

                                                    2010048335

Printed by Bethany Press in Bloomington, MN – 04/11

                    1 3 5 7 9 10 8 6 4 2

Printed in the United States of America

For
My Paternal Aunt
Ruth Perry Hart
(August 29, 1944)

What a blessing to have a spunky aunt like you.
You've always taught me to tell it like it is.
Thank you for opening up and revealing
your life lessons to me.
I heard you loud and clear, and I'm hanging
in there because of your wisdom.
I pray every reader learns the principle
of this book and decides like you . . .
to stand up for what's right even
if you have to stand alone!

Morgan Love Series

Contents

Chapter 1
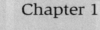
All Better

"Where are you going? I just know you don't think you're going with us, Morgan." My new cousin Drake, who was my stepdaddy's nephew, was acting like I had the **plague** or something.

Placing my hands on my hips, I said back with attitude, "Yes, I'm going. That's why I'm getting my coat. Can you tell Daddy Derek to hold on a second, please?"

Since it was December, I also needed to grab my gloves and hat to keep warm. Just as I was heading quickly to my room, I felt somebody behind me stepping on my heel. I knew it was that rude Drake, and he didn't even say that he was sorry.

"No. I won't tell him that," Drake said, as he continued to follow me.

"Ouch!" I yelled out. I turned to face him after he stepped on my heel a second time. "What's your problem?"

Drake jumped in front of me so I couldn't move. "You need to stay home. Okay? This is a time for me and my uncle to spend together. It's called 'man time.' We're going to the hardware store to get some paint, and that's not a place for girls. Just stay here and wait for my sisters to wake up. Maybe y'all can bake cupcakes, or Christmas cookies, or something."

"He doesn't even know what color I want for my room, Drake. Get out of my way because I'm going," I told him, as I pushed him to the side and went into my room.

"Ugh! You're always ruining stuff," Drake huffed, as he came into my room uninvited.

"What do you mean?" I asked.

I was in shock. I couldn't believe it. Of all people, Drake was the one to talk about me messing up something? This was my first Christmas with my new brother and my new stepdad in our new house. And, because of him and his sisters, we weren't alone. My new cousins were staying with us, and they were crowding my space.

Drake, who was two years older than me, was a pain worse than a loose tooth being pulled out. Samantha, who liked to be called Sam, was ten. She thought she was the next Teen Miss America. At first I used to admire how cute she always looked. But when she started taking up extra time in the bathroom every day, her primping was not cool. Sadie was a year older than me and we got along just fine.

The only thing was, she liked playing with dolls all the time. There were more things that I wanted to do, that I wanted to try, and that I wanted to learn.

"Just forget about tagging along, I told you. He knows what color pink to get for your room. Your mom wrote it all down. Now we're ready to go and we figured out everything last night when we talked about our 'man plan' for today. You were nowhere in it, Morgan. Stay home!" Drake headed out of my room and slammed the door.

I backed into my bed and sat on it. My feelings at the time told me to put both of my hands under my chin and pout. I wanted to cry, but because I was a big girl, I decided not to.

I couldn't do anything. I sure was mad at the fact that Drake was going with Daddy Derek and I wasn't. At Thanksgiving dinner, Drake had been feeling **insecure** about not having his uncle in his life the way he wanted now that Daddy Derek had a new family. So I was the one who went out of my way to make Drake feel special.

And now that I wanted to be included in what they were doing, he didn't want me to be. And that wasn't fair. It wasn't really okay, but I had to tell myself that so the tears wouldn't come. I was holding them back pretty hard.

● ● ● ● ●

The only thing I could do was wait until Daddy Derek came back. Then we could have some special time of our own. Now, three hours had passed and I was becoming

impatient. I mean, what did they have to do, mix the paint too? Did they get lost trying to find the paint store?

Fifteen minutes later, I learned that wasn't the case because the two of them walked into the house with smiling faces. They had bags filled with items to do work in the yard and the house, along with tons of paint.

Daddy Derek called me over to see the paint sample for my room. When I saw the pretty shade of pink he bought, my mouth stretched with excitement from ear to ear. But then my smile quickly dropped when I wondered if I were going to be able to help paint it. If not, I wouldn't enjoy my room as much.

I followed Daddy Derek outside. "I can help you guys."

"Thank you, sweetheart, but I don't want you to have to do any heavy lifting. Drake and I can handle it. You go on back inside and help your mom," Daddy Derek said, patting me on the head.

Drake looked over at me and stuck out his tongue. I wanted to yank it, but I just walked back into the house. I thought about my dad, my real dad, who was serving our country in the U.S. Navy off the coast of Africa. I missed him so much, and I knew that if he were here, then he would let me help. Daddy always told me that girls could do anything guys can do. There were women serving in the Navy with him.

What did Daddy Derek think would happen? That I would break a nail or something? I was strong and just needed a way to prove it.

Throughout the day, I was told no every time I wanted to help. I couldn't help put up the fence. I couldn't help spread the pine straw. I couldn't help plant the flowers. I couldn't help organize the shelves in the garage. I couldn't help. I couldn't help. I couldn't help! What was the big deal? I wasn't going to get hurt or anything.

Pretty soon I got tired of trying and just gave up. The minute I walked in the house, Mom sent me right back out to get the mail.

Walking past the guys, I saw they were sweating from head to toe from all the hard work they were doing. Daddy Derek looked at me and said, "Hey, Morgan. I know you're glad you're not out here working this hard." I just stared at him.

"Uncle Derek, I'm thirsty," Drake said.

"Morgan, can you go and grab us a couple bottles of water?" Daddy Derek said to me, as if all I was good for was being the maid.

I ran to the mailbox to get the mail and went back inside. Mom was tending to Jayden so I laid the mail on the table beside her. Then I went to the kitchen and opened the refrigerator to grab the two waters. Running back outside, I handed one to Daddy Derek. I really wanted to throw Drake's water at his head because he had a smirk on his face. He was probably thinking that since I was a girl I had to be his servant, but I gave him the water anyway. It just made me so mad. I walked away feeling worse than a kid nobody wants on their team.

Later that night at dinner, I said nothing. My parents and cousins were talking so much they didn't need to hear my voice anyway. As soon as I was done eating, I asked to be excused from the table. Mom had taught me good manners so I asked if I could leave the table instead of just getting up and walking away.

A few minutes went by and Mom came up to my room. She looked at the finished walls and said, "Morgan, the paint smell is too strong. You don't need to sleep in here tonight. Your room looks great, though. Do you like it? I think it's a bold pink, but it's cute."

In an **uninterested** way, I said, "It's okay, Mom."

"Okay? Morgan you've been wanting this color for weeks. What's wrong? I know it's a lot having three extra kids around your age in the house, but it'll work out."

"I know, Mom. Their mother is a single parent, and she wanted to get away for the holidays. I understand that our present to her is to keep her kids. I'm fine with it and that's not what's bothering me."

"Well, what is bothering you?" she asked, stepping closer to me.

I stepped away from her. She was my mom and parents were supposed to know all about their kids—forward and backward. She must have seen me all day asking to help Daddy Derek and Drake. A part of me thought she'd tell Daddy Derek to let me help. But she didn't. And because I didn't wanna cause any **friction** between them, I just told her what she wanted to hear.

I said it again. "I'm okay, Mom. Just tired. Everything is cool." I said it, knowing deep in my heart it wasn't true.

• • • • •

The neighborhood we moved into was new and we were the first family to stay there. When we saw a moving truck parked outside, we got excited at the thought of new neighbors. My mom was thrilled to think she might find a new buddy and I was hoping they had kids my age. She had told me not too long ago that the **recession** was turning around and more people were starting to buy new homes.

When Mom and Daddy Derek went down the street to greet the family, Sadie turned to me and said, "I guess you're bummed out, huh?"

"Why do you say that?"

"I know you were hoping for them to have daughters but they've got boys." She twisted her face as if boys had diseases.

I really just wanted them to have kids, period. I didn't need any other girlfriends because I had Brooke and Chanté at school and Sadie and Sam at home. I did want to have some adventure and play outside more. Sometimes girls don't want to play rough. I don't mean wrestling or anything like that. Just somebody to play a game of kickball with or go bike riding with. When I saw the two boys running around with a soccer ball, I wanted to go over even more.

"Let's go and meet them," I said.

Sam said, "You guys can go on. I need to curl my hair."

"But Mom said you're not supposed to curl your hair, Sam," Sadie said.

"Well, Mom's not here, is she?" Sam snapped back at her younger sister.

Drake, Sadie, and I walked a couple of houses down to meet the new neighbors.

"Oh, and here comes our crew now," I heard Daddy Derek say. "This is our daughter, Morgan, and our niece and nephew, Drake and Sadie. Where's Sam?"

"Don't ask," Sadie said, rolling her eyes.

Daddy Derek laughed. "We have an older niece too, Samantha. Guys, meet the London family." Pointing at the boys, he said, "These are their sons, Antoine and Alec. You all should stay out here and play for a while."

"Yeah, but not too much longer. I'm sure they need their boys to help them move some things around," Mom added.

"I don't mind helping," I said before Daddy Derek cut in.

"Morgan, I'm sure they've got it. You just play for a while and get to know each other a bit."

I don't think he knew how much that comment hurt my feelings. Why did he think I couldn't do anything?

"Can y'all play dodge ball?" the older boy asked.

"Yeah," Drake, Sadie, and I all answered at once.

"Well, it was nice meeting you folks. We should get together soon," Mom said. Then all the grownups left us alone.

All of a sudden, the two boys, who seemed nice when their parents were around, turned into animals. Antoine picked up the ball and threw it hard at Drake's head.

"Ow! We're not even ready yet," Drake said.

Antoine yelled, "Ah, come on! What are you, a wimp or something? I know that didn't hurt."

"No, it didn't hurt," Drake said, rubbing the side of his head. "I just wasn't ready. That's all."

When Sadie saw Alec and Antoine jumping up and down like they couldn't wait to hit us even harder with the ball, she said, "I don't wanna play this game. You guys play too rough."

"Let's play! If you can't stand the heat then you better get out of the game," Antoine called out.

Sadie sat on the curbside and started cheering us on. I was ready to take them on and was dodging all of their balls. It was easy enough because it didn't seem like they were throwing them at me too hard. But they were trying to hurt Drake for real.

Then, Alec threw the ball at Drake's face and hit him in the eye. He yelled, "Touchdown!" as Drake stumbled and fell to the ground.

"Wait a minute. We're not playing football," I said to Alec.

Antoine said, "Y'all are playing whatever we wanna play. I told you if you couldn't stand it, then get out of the game. You decided to stay in, so deal with it."

"I'm not dealing with nothin'," Drake said, as he tried to

get up. But Antoine pressed his foot down hard on Drake's chest.

I was really getting mad at my cousin. He was the one who kept saying girls couldn't do this and girls couldn't do that. But now he had his hands full because he had run into some really bad boys. It wasn't right how rough they were playing. And I knew I should help my cousin out and not let them mess with Drake.

"Get your foot off him!" I yelled.

"Man, you've gotta have that little girl take up for you because you can't take up for yourself. I told you, Alec, before he walked over here, that he was a girl," Antoine teased.

"For your information—" I started to say before Drake grabbed me.

He'd had enough and was pulling me toward the house. "Stop! I'm talking to them. I don't need you to defend me. Okay?" he said.

"I'm trying to help you. I'm going right in there and telling my mom," I said.

"No, you're not," Drake said, as he stood in front of me and looked at me with a very mean face. "Did you hear what those guys just said to me? They called me a girl. Man! I didn't even wanna come here for Christmas anyway."

I watched Drake walk faster. And even after how he treated me, I was sorry he felt so bad. Maybe I shouldn't have said anything to help him. I really didn't know how to make it all better, but what I tried to do wasn't helping.

● ● ● ● ●

"Morgan, we thought you wouldn't ever want to come back over here. With all those kids and the loads of fun you're having at your house," Papa joked, "I just knew you'd forgotten about your old grandpa."

He didn't know how happy I was to be spending the day with my grandparents on Christmas Eve. I bet it did seem like fun to have three other kids in the house, but that was far from the truth.

Sam didn't wanna play at all. She just primped in front of the mirror all day long like her beauty was going to change any second. Every chance she got she was worrying about her long, black hair and making sure that her lip gloss was shiny enough.

Drake didn't wanna play with me, thinking it would make him look bad. He was still upset about what happened with the new boys down the street, so he just played alone. Sadie and I could talk about a lot of things, but I was tired of making the Barbie dolls talk. I was tired of playing house. Sadie loved helping my mom with baby Jayden, and my mom liked having a helper who was **enthusiastic**.

Every time Mama and Papa asked if I could come over, my mom would tell them I had company. Finally, after begging her to take me over to see my grandparents, she finally dropped me off. Mom could tell I needed the break, but I couldn't stay overnight. Though my visit was only for the day, it was still fun for me. Mama and Papa were like my best buddies, and I had missed them.

"Your mom will be here to get you soon, young lady."

Papa was pleased that we had done a lot together and asked me, "Did you enjoy going to the movies and shopping at the mall? Did you have fun playing board games?" He really made me feel good, knowing all the things that I liked to do. "Anything for my baby girl," he said.

"Papa, can you call my mom and tell her I don't wanna go home?"

Mama had been listening, but when she heard me say that, she slid over next to me. Putting her arm around my neck, she said, "Okay. You don't wanna go home and this is Christmas Eve. Why? What's going on?"

I didn't say anything. "Is anybody hurting you, Morgan?" Papa said, looking concerned.

I knew I had to speak up then because he was ready to grab his coat and keys to head over there. "No, I'm okay. I'm fine."

"That's not an 'I'm fine' sound," Mama replied. "How about I bake some cookies before your mom comes and we can talk about it?"

"Okay," I said in a sad tone, like I'd lost my favorite toy.

Mama was a really good cook and her desserts were the best. Soon I had some delicious warm cookies set on a plate in front of me. My eyes grew big when I saw the shapes of Christmas trees, reindeer, and crosses, all dazzled with red and green colored sprinkles. Mama knew just how to get me to open up.

"Tell us, Morgan. You know we can talk about any-thing. It must be rough with all those kids over there. Are they getting in your way? Are they bullying you? What's wrong, baby?"

"Oh," I huffed. "It's just . . . "

"What? It would've been a nicer Christmas if y'all would've been by yourselves, wouldn't it?" Papa said as Mama poked him. "I told my daughter it wasn't a good idea to let Derek's nieces and nephew come over there on y'all's first Christmas as a family. That's a lot on everybody."

"Hush up, now!" Mama told him.

"Papa, do you remember how you let me meet your coworkers that day?"

"Yep, I sure do. A lot of my coworkers are still talking about how little Morgan has such good manners. It makes me so proud to hear that."

"And how about when you let me help you fix things around here?"

"Yeah. I gotta show you how to do stuff like I did with your mom."

"Well, that's just it. Daddy Derek doesn't let me do anything. He looks at me like I'm some little girl that could break her hand whenever I try to help do things. Drake is getting on my nerves. He wants all of Daddy Derek's time because he doesn't have a dad of his own. Sure, it's okay for them to spend time together, but Drake doesn't wanna share. Sometimes I think Mommy doesn't want me to have any fun! I'm a girl, and I like being a girl, but girls can do lots of things. I don't wanna just sit around painting my nails all day long like Sam."

"Tell that to your grandma," Papa whispered.

"Hush," Mama snapped.

I looked at both of them. "I'm serious."

All of a sudden, Mommy walked into the kitchen and picked up on what we were saying, "You're serious about what? Morgan, are you ready to go? I don't have much time. Ooh, Mom, you baked cookies," she said, grabbing one. Just like that she stopped rushing and sat down next to me.

They were so good with milk. But I was too upset to eat more right then. I had to tell Mom what was on my mind.

"Mommy, may I spend the night?" I asked.

Mama spoke first, "Yes, maybe she should stay here because she's telling us some things that we need to address."

No, no, no, I thought to myself. I wanted Mama to stop talking. My grandparents knew the rule: whatever we talked about stayed between us. And now they were going to break it.

"This is very important though, Morgan," Mama said.

Mom asked, "What did Morgan tell you?"

"She just feels left out because she's not allowed to help out around the house. And you and your husband need to know that Morgan likes to help," Mama said.

My mom looked at me and said, "Oh, Morgan, I didn't

know you wanted to help out. Why didn't you say something?"

"I didn't think I had to, Mom. That's my room, and you know I wanted to paint it. Helping with the work is part of the fun. What I didn't wanna tell you is that Drake was saying Daddy Derek didn't want me to help. I just didn't want there to be any problems."

"Sometimes you gotta talk about things. Sometimes you need to open up, and that's okay. You're not being a tattletale when you express your feelings. We can't fix something when we don't know something is wrong. We love you, Morgan. Don't feel like you have to keep anything from me," Mom said and kissed my cheek. "Daddy Derek does like having you around to help him."

Papa whispered to me, "See, we had to tell. Now everything will be all better."

Letter to Dad

Dear Dad,

Sometimes boys can be mean and they treat girls like we have the **plague**. Is it that some boys are **insecure** because girls may be stronger than them? Well, whatever it is, I'm getting **impatient** with boys thinking they can push me around. I can play dodge ball and football. And I'm **uninterested** in playing with Barbie dolls all day, though I do want a new doll for Christmas. I just wish you were here to help me with the **friction** between me and my cousin Drake. I do feel **sorry** for him because his mom has to work two jobs to make up for the one she lost because of the **recession**. Pray for us because we're not that **enthusiastic** to be around each other.

> Your daughter,
> Tough Girl, Morgan

Word Search

```
U  M  F  S  I  L  V  E  R  N  O  C
C  N  R  P  E  O  X  Y  G  E  I  G
H  C  I  N  A  U  T  A  B  T  M  O
E  A  C  N  E  H  G  A  S  L  P  L
I  R  T  L  T  O  N  A  N  M  A  D
N  B  I  E  P  E  I  T  L  E  T  C
S  O  O  A  Q  S  R  R  S  P  I  O
E  N  N  D  U  Z  K  E  A  Y  E  P
C  O  Z  H  Z  I  N  C  S  O  N  P
U  E  T  A  R  G  O  N  D  T  T  E
R  N  E  N  O  I  S  S  E  C  E  R
E  H  Y  D  R  O  G  E  N  L  N  D
```

ENTHUSIASTIC

FRICTION

IMPATIENT

INSECURE

PLAGUE

RECESSION

UNINTERESTED

Words to Know and Learn

1) **plague** (plāg) *noun*
A widespread affliction or calamity

2) **in·se·cure** (ĭn'sĭ-kyʊr') *adjective*
Not sure or certain; doubtful

3) **im·pa·tient** (ĭm-pā'shənt) *adjective*
Unable to wait patiently or tolerate delay; restless

4) **un·in·ter·est·ed** (ŭn-ĭn'trĭ-stĭd) *adjective*
Without an interest in a particular thing

5) **fric·tion** (frĭk'shən) *noun*
Conflict; disagreement between people or groups of people

6) **re·ces·sion** (rĭ-sĕsh'ən) *noun*
A period of reduced or declining economic activity

7) **en·thu·si·as·tic** (ĕn-thū'zē-ăs'tĭk) *adjective*
Having or showing great interest

Chapter 2
Too Cool

"Wow! Look at all my presents!" I was so excited, as I ran downstairs to the family room. My gifts were piled high next to the pretty, white Christmas tree. "Are these all for me?"

I counted the boxes and couldn't believe there were twenty-five presents with my name on them. "From: Santa, To: Morgan Noelle Love," the pretty tags read. Big boxes. Shiny boxes. Long boxes. Short boxes—I was so happy!

It had been a rough year for me. I had to say good-bye to my dad. I had to adjust to a new dad. My mom and baby brother had been sick, and I was scared I would lose them. And I had to make new friends at a new school. It was one thing after another, but seeing those gifts made the end of my year look great.

After looking over my huge stash, I didn't even care about what my cousins or anyone else got. I just yelled out,

"Mom, can I open my gifts now?" Before she could give an answer, I had ripped off a bow and was halfway through the shiny wrapping paper.

"Ooh, Morgan, that Barbie doll is so pretty," Sadie said. "Look at her outfits and her hair. May I see her?"

I handed the doll to her and went on to the next thing. This box was long and wrapped pretty tight. Using all my muscles, I opened it to find a new guitar. I would surely get around to playing with it, just not right away. As I searched around trying to decide which box I would open next, out of the corner of my eye, I watched Drake eyeing my guitar.

"Do you wanna see it?" I asked him.

"Oh, yeah! A guitar was on my list too," Drake said, as he reached for it with a big smile on his face.

"Here, you can play it," I said, handing it to him.

The next present was a cute and girly box. It was small enough for a ring or something like that. Opening it up, there was a pretty gold necklace with matching earrings inside. Sam started to oooh and aaah over the jewelry. I knew it was the type of stuff she liked, so I let her see them.

I kept on tearing open presents until pieces of wrapping paper were everywhere. I was so lost in my own world that I hadn't realized my cousins were watching me. They only had two presents each—one from their mom and one from my parents. So their eyes were on me because they didn't have any more gifts to open.

That was too bad, but it wasn't my fault! I had gifts

from Mama and Papa. Of course, Daddy sent me some things from overseas. Mommy and Daddy Derek gave me a bunch of stuff. And even the Navy had sent me a gift. I had lots of wonderful things, and I loved them all!

I was down to the last five boxes to open and one envelope. Inside the envelope, I found five $20 bills. That was $100! "Yea!" I squealed. "I got some money! I can buy myself some more things!" I shouted.

When I started dancing around and singing, "I got a guitar. I got a new doll. I got a necklace. I got a—" All of a sudden, Mom snatched me from the family room and pulled me into the bathroom. "What are you doing, Morgan?" she asked making sure to not let me leave the bathroom.

"What, Mom? I'm just enjoying my Christmas. Thank you so much!" I reached up, trying to wrap my arms around her. But she wasn't having it.

"No, you're bragging, Morgan Love. And I don't like that." She looked disappointed.

"Bragging about what?" I asked, not sure what she meant.

"Sweetheart, didn't you see your cousins' faces?"

I shook my head. "No, I was checking out my stuff."

"Baby, you're a person who cares about other people's feelings. Right?"

I nodded yes.

"That's why you have to be aware when people around you are hurting. If I would've had the money to buy them more gifts, then I would have," Mom explained. "But we bought your gifts long before we knew they were coming."

She sounded upset when she said, "I told Derek not to have you open all of your gifts at once."

"What, you wanted to keep some of my presents away from me because they wouldn't have as many?" I asked with my voice turning sad.

She sighed. "It's not that you wouldn't have gotten them at all, sweetie. You just didn't need them all today. I **predicted** this might happen," Mom said in a worried way.

"I don't understand, Mom," I said, folding my arms and poking out my lips.

She went on. "I mean, I saw this coming. While you're all excited about what the Lord blessed you with, your cousins weren't given as much, and they're not happy."

"Well, why didn't they get more stuff? Weren't they good?"

Mom walked around in a circle and scratched her head. "Morgan, I'm sure they were good. Sometimes we just don't always get all we desire. But I need you to remember this. The Lord was the One who allowed those gifts to be here this morning for you. But when people aren't as fortunate, we don't need to rub it in their faces. I'm not saying it's your fault they're in this situation. I just don't want us to be the cause of them not having a great day. Do you understand?"

"Yes, ma'am, I get it now."

We left the bathroom and went back to the family

room. Mom was right all along. I could tell when I saw their long faces.

"Okay, everyone, let's eat breakfast," Mom said, trying to take their mind off their sadness and make them smile.

But even with the wonderful spread of pancakes, waffles, French toast, scrambled eggs, bacon, sausage, and ham that she had fixed for us, it still didn't cheer them up. When I tried to talk to them, none of them had anything to say.

I had learned a big lesson in the wrong way. You have to be **conscious** of other people's feelings and never brag. You just don't know when you could hurt someone's feelings, even when you don't intend to. But I was growing and learning. Now I knew.

● ● ● ● ●

My cousins tried to ignore me most of Christmas day on purpose. Even though I was being nice and not playing with my own stuff, they were still leaving me out. After all, I did let Sam try on my new necklace. Drake got to play with my new guitar. And I let Sadie play with my new doll. I wanted to be the first one to try out all my things and enjoy Christmas, but I wasn't. I did **sacrifice**, and I did share. But that wasn't enough for them.

I was downstairs watching the Disney Christmas parade by myself and Daddy Derek came and sat beside me. "Hey, Morgan, are you okay?"

"Yes, I'm fine," I said, feeling sad and knowing he wasn't buying it.

"Your mom told me she fussed at you. I hope you see that you have a little more than my sister's kids. I'm sorry you're sad on Christmas. I think that you should be able to enjoy your things even though the other kids are here. It's okay for you to play with your stuff, Morgan. I want you to enjoy it."

"Okay," I said with a tiny smile.

I was glad that he did care about how I felt, but Mom was right. My cousins were here whether anyone liked it or not. I couldn't believe how mad they were at me because of all the gifts I got. Since we only had a couple more days until they went home, I would tough it out and let them play with my things.

"Know what? Maybe a little fresh air is what everyone needs," Daddy Derek said, thinking he had a great plan to bring peace to the house.

"No, I'm fine, honest. I don't want you to make them play with me."

Daddy Derek smiled at me and yelled out, "Drake!"

"Yes, sir?"

"Get yourself on down here right now. Bring your shoes and your sisters. Y'all are going outside to play with Morgan."

Drake was the first one down. He just looked at me and frowned. "But—"

"Did you 'but' me, boy?" Daddy Derek said in a strong voice.

Drake could tell he wasn't playing, and said, "Okay, we're going."

We all put on our coats, hats, and gloves. Walking outside, I actually thought this could be a cool way for us to let go of some of the early morning **tension** and just have fun. I would go along with anything they wanted to do, but it needed to be something we could all enjoy.

Looking around the garage to get some ideas, I spotted my red ball on the garage floor. I asked them, "You wanna play dodge ball?"

"I'll throw it," Sam spoke first. "I'm trying not to run back and forth. I might slip and get dirty."

"You're not going to slip," I told Sam.

Sadie leaned close to me and joked, "Oh, then you don't know my sister. She's got two left feet." And we laughed and it felt good.

Drake, of course, was the one who wanted to hit somebody with the ball. He got on the opposite side of Sam and threw the first pass. It didn't surprise me that he aimed it right at me, but I dodged it.

Then Sam picked up the ball and threw it. Not at Sadie, but at me—hard. She missed me by a long shot, but her face told me that she was trying to take me down.

"You guys can't get me. I'm too good at this. This must be my day!" I teased.

"Yeah, it is your day," Drake said. "Do you have to keep going on and on about all that stuff you got for Christmas?"

"Yeah," Sam said. "You know we're only playing with you because Uncle Derek said we had to."

Drake took the ball and aimed it at me again. He threw it extra hard in my direction and this time he tagged me. I slipped and fell in the mud. Sam and Drake started laughing really hard. They even came over to where I was and stood over me, laughing.

"Ouch!" I screamed because it hurt really badly when I fell. The ground rubbed against my leg and it was burning even through my pant leg. They were actually thinking it was funny to see me in pain.

Sadie was the only one who was nice to me. She came over and put out her hand to help me up. As soon as I was up, I yanked my hand from her and ran away.

I kept walking until I went way past my house. All I could think was I wanted to get as far from them as I could. *Lord,* I prayed, *I'm trying. This is hard though. This isn't what I wanted for my Christmas. I'm just a little girl, and I don't get everything right the first time, but why does this have to be so hard? Why do they have to be mad at me? Why can't they just leave? I let them play with my toys and they still don't like me. They think I'm a brat. Well, maybe I should just be a brat then. Can You please help me?*

They didn't even try and stop me. I had gone so far from my house that I was in a part of the **subdivision** where the houses weren't finished yet. All I could see was woods in front of me, but I didn't dare go in. Then I heard some crying and shouting and it just didn't sound right. So

I stepped a little closer to the trees. To my surprise, I was shocked to see Antoine punching Alec in the stomach real hard. But when he heard me coming, Antoine jetted away like a plane taking off.

I rushed over to Alec and said, "Are you okay? Let's go home and tell your dad. Your brother needs to get in trouble. Why is he so mean?"

Alec stopped holding his stomach and grabbed my coat collar. "Leave me alone, you girl! You'd better not say anything or the same thing will happen to you. You got that?" He let me go and ran away.

I was still shocked at what had happened. It wasn't cool at all and even worse, Alec scared me. Did he really mean that he'd hurt me if I said something? I had just told Mom I wouldn't keep secrets from her, but now I was afraid. As I walked home thinking about it, I knew I couldn't tell on those two brothers. No telling what they might do. One thing I did know, even if someone made me mad again, I knew I wasn't going to wander that far away anymore.

Huffing and puffing all the way home, I prayed out loud, "Lord, did You hear me? My day isn't getting any better, it's getting worse."

It seemed like I had been away for a long time, but that was probably because I was pretty shook up.

When I walked up the street, my cousins were still playing in front of my house. They didn't say anything to me and no one inside seemed to notice that I had been gone. All I could think was, *I'm glad I made it home in one piece.*

• • • • •

The next day was Sunday and we were at church. I didn't have to be an usher today, so I got to sit right next to Mom and baby Jayden. Daddy Derek worked at the church, so he couldn't sit with us. We sat on the front row near the First Lady. Mom told me that I had to sit up straight, pay attention, and be on my best behavior. I wanted to make sure to do what she said for me to do.

I was listening very hard to Rev. Barney this morning. These past few days had been rough and I needed to hear some good news to help get me through the bad times. It didn't matter that I'm just a young girl; I still wanted so badly to be closer to God. Papa always said people come to church to get fed so that was what I wanted to do. I told myself that I would feed on God's Word so I could be happy.

Rev. Barney was saying, "Well, yesterday was Christmas. And if your house was anything like mine, which I'm pretty sure it was, the kids got up early and ran straight past the breakfast table to get to their presents."

So far I thought he was right, and I kept listening. "Even we adults were excited to open up something from our loved ones, coworkers, and friends. I can hear you complaining now: *Why did she give me this? I got something better than that from her last year.* Or: *Why did he get me that?*"

He had the whole church laughing, as he imitated the adults and their selfish behavior.

Rev. Barney went on talking. "I'm sure a lot of grumbling was going on, and a lot of people were caught up in the wrong things. They weren't interested in the *one thing* that mattered most about yesterday."

Mom squeezed my hand. I didn't know why, but I squeezed hers back. She gave me a look that said, *listen closely.* I was already trying to keep my focus on what Rev. Barney was talking about because I wanted to understand what that "one thing" was.

"See, Christmas isn't about the gifts under the tree. It is about the gift God gave us—His only begotten Son, Jesus— who died for us to be saved. You see, when you're caught up in God's Son, Jesus Christ, it doesn't matter if you didn't get the earthly present you wanted. It doesn't matter if you got all the things you wanted in the world, and other people were disappointed in their presents. It doesn't even matter if you didn't get anything at all. Do you know why?"

Some of the church members said out loud, "Why?" And that included me. Then Rev. Barney said, "Because when you're excited and filled with thoughts of Jesus and understanding that He is the greatest gift in life, then no other thing can compare or should matter."

Rev. Barney stepped down from the **pulpit** and walked down the aisle. He was looking over the congregation to make sure we didn't miss what he was trying to say. I watched as everyone nodded at him and paid attention. I understood a little of what he was saying, but I was waiting for more. I think we all were waiting for more.

"You see, even us grown folks get it wrong sometimes. We get so caught up in wanting to receive something, that we fail to accept the gift that's already been given to us. And we fail to give something back. The Lord wants us to show Him that we are thankful. Not for what He will do for us, but for what He already has done. The church administrator, Derek Randall, told me that his daughter, Morgan, learned the slogan WWJD: 'What Would Jesus Do?' in Sunday school. Sometimes he hears her around the house saying it. And it sounds so cute and sweet."

Okay, by then I was feeling a little uncomfortable that he was talking about me. I didn't want him to make me an example. Why couldn't he talk about someone else? People were looking all around trying to find me, so I ducked down under my mom. I didn't want him talking about me, even if it was only for a little while.

"If little Morgan can think about what Jesus would do in certain situations, then you know we adults should do that too. But I'm talking to everybody—grown-ups and kids too. No, you might not have gotten what you wanted for Christmas. But would Jesus be mad about it, or would He be happy that He got something? Yes, you got a gift that was better than someone else's, but would Jesus share His things or would He keep them all to Himself?

"There are a lot of unfortunate people who don't have food and shelter. Would Jesus share His food? Would He go out and **volunteer**? Come on, people. Your lives may not be perfect, but that's only part of the story. And it's not the most important part."

By then, I was a little lost. What is the most important

part? What is Christmas really about?

He continued, "When you know the King of kings and the Lord of lords, and you understand that He allowed His Son to leave His side and be born for you, then you'll be complete. Do you love the Lord? Are you truly thankful for Jesus? Then get on your feet and thank Him. Not for sending you presents—but for giving you the best gift. He sent His Son to be born for you."

People were standing up and shouting. The sound was getting louder than a crowd at a football game. It was amazing. And for the first time, I felt myself raise my hand up in the air as I said, "Thank You, Lord!"

The next thing I knew, Drake leaned over and said, "Morgan, we're sorry for being mean to you yesterday. Are we cool?" I could see his sisters looking over and smiling at me too. I could tell they were sorry, and so was I. All of us had been paying attention to the wrong things. Of course, I forgave them. God had answered my cry for help after all.

Now I understand what Christmas is really about. Yesterday, I had been happy to see all those boxes that were for me, but that feeling didn't even compare to how happy I was to know that God allowed Jesus to be born because He loves me so much. Getting new things was neat. But God's love for me is the coolest thing of all. Too cool!

Letter to Dad

Dear Dad,

   Christmas day was just okay. Mom said she **predicted** there couild be hurt feelings because I got the most gifts. She was right. I was so happy to see all you sent me, and I wasn't **conscious** that my cousins didn't have much. I did **sacrifice** playing with my new things, and I let them play with them instead. Even so, we still had **tension** all day.

   A few days ago some rough boys moved into our **subdivision**. I'll tell you more about them later.

   Today was much better. Church was awesome. Rev. Barney was in the **pulpit** and told us about the true meaning of Christmas. It's about giving and not receiving. I'm glad you **volunteered** to join the Navy and serve our country. Dad, you give all the time, and I love you. Be safe.

Your daughter,
Thankful, Morgan

Word Search

```
V  F  O  U  R  S  C  O  R  E  N  M
O  W  H  E  N  I  N  N  J  O  O  C
L  A  N  D  T  H  E  S  I  A  I  C
U  S  E  V  E  N  R  S  K  L  S  O
N  R  P  U  L  P  I  T  J  C  N  N
T  A  G  O  W  V  K  X  B  X  E  S
E  C  I  F  I  R  C  A  S  R  T  C
E  Z  D  D  Y  E  A  R  S  D  Z  I
R  W  B  C  O  U  R  S  E  O  F  O
A  U  P  R  E  D  I  C  T  E  D  U
S  E  V  E  N  T  S  H  U  M  E  S
R  E  V  B  A  R  N  E  Y  T  O  O
```

CONSCIOUS

PREDICTED

PULPIT

SACRIFICE

SUBDIVISION

TENSION

VOLUNTEER

Words to Know and Learn

1) pre·dict·ed (prĭ-dĭkt'ed) *verb*
Said ahead of time that something would happen

2) con·scious (kŏn'shəs) *adjective*
Sensitive to; knowing; aware (often followed by "of")

3) sac·ri·fice (săk'rə-fīs') *noun*
The act of giving something up

4) ten·sion (tĕn'shən) *noun*
Mental, emotional, or nervous strain

5) sub·di·vi·sion (sŭb'dĭ-vĭzh'ən, sŭb'dĭ-vĭzh'ənn) *noun*
A large area of real estate land divided into smaller lots

6) pul·pit (pʊl'pĭt, pŭl'-) *noun*
The raised platform or stand used in preaching or conducting a religious service

7) vol·un·teer (vŏl'ən-tîr') *verb*
To offer to perform a service

Chapter 3

Can't Tell

"Morgan! There you are, girl. I missed you," Brooke said, waving me down.

It was the first day back to school after winter break. I just knew it was going to be a great day. I put down my pink flowered book bag and ran straight to Brooke. I had missed her so much. Her family was out of town over the break, so I didn't get to see or talk to her the whole time. I couldn't wait for us to be best buddies again.

"So, how was your Christmas?" Brooke said to me after we hugged each other tight.

"It was okay," I said, thinking about the fact that my cousins made it rough. But then I thought about the sermon Rev. Barney preached on Sunday. "No, I take that back, girl. It was really good, and I hope yours was too."

"It was, and I'm glad to see you again, girlfriend!"

Chanté stood over in a corner behind Brooke, almost

like she was scared to join us. It was crazy. This was a new season, and I thought we were past all of the drama. I mean, all of us were supposed to be buddies and hang out together—us girls and even crazy Trey.

I said to Brooke, "Let's go over and talk to Chanté."

"Okay, cool. Let's go."

Chanté was smiling when we got closer to her. I spoke first. "Hey, Chanté, you wanna walk to class with us?"

Suddenly, the smile on her face turned to a frown.

Brooke looked over and saw Trey and said, "I'll be right back."

I could tell something was bothering her, and I asked, "Chanté, what's the matter? Why do you look so sad? Are you worried that we all won't be friends? Don't worry, we're gonna get along."

"I just don't think Brooke likes me. I don't know." Chanté hung her head down again.

Touching her shoulder to pep her up, I said, "Don't be **paranoid**, Chanté. Brooke thinks you're cool. You just have to get over acting shy. Okay?"

"But I'm not like you, Morgan. Everyone likes you. You're a leader."

"Come on, girl. I've gone through hard stuff when no one wanted to talk to me. And, believe me, that didn't feel good. I wouldn't want anyone else to feel that way either. Let's just all get along."

"Yeah, okay," Chanté said shyly as Trey and Brooke headed back over to us.

"What's up, Morgan?" Trey said.

"What's up, Trey!" I said back.

All the bad feelings between us from before were gone. We played around and slapped hands and traded Christmas stories. I told them about my long break with my cousins. Brooke told us her story about her new dog. Trey shared stories about his grandparents. And Chanté just listened to everything. We were gonna have to work on her shyness.

As we headed into our classroom, everyone was happy to see Miss Nelson. That is, until she told us our first assignment. We had to write a paragraph about how we spent our Christmas break. A lot of sighs were heard around the room. But since I was used to writing my dad letters, I was okay with it and was ready to get my work done.

The teacher wrote on the board that our paper had to have a main topic sentence, three sentences to back up the main sentence, and a closing sentence. It was only about five lines, and everybody but me was upset.

"Come on, y'all. We just talked about this. We can do this," I said to Brooke and Trey. They both nodded and we went to work.

My first sentence was: "I learned that Christmas is what you make of it."

Before I could move on to my next three sentences, Miss Nelson said, "Okay class, I need you all to stop for just a minute. We have a new student."

Just hearing the words "new student" made me ready to listen. It was time for me to step up and help a new student feel welcome. I knew what it was like to be the new kid and how frightening it can be. If people were more welcoming at this school, then newcomers wouldn't have anything to worry about.

"You know what?" Miss Nelson said. "Go ahead and finish your paragraph first. I'll be right back in after I speak to the new boy's parents. You have ten minutes left to get it done."

"Man, just when I thought we were off the hook," Trey said in a joking way.

Everybody laughed, including me. I looked over at Trey and gave him a "thumbs up" and he gave me one back. He already knew that I could get my work done, but I was counting on him to finish too. We were cool and I was on his side. In his own way, Trey was trying to be a leader. He got the class to quiet down and start writing.

After my topic sentence, my first point was: "I had to share my house with my three cousins. Though it wasn't all fun, it was a blessing to have a bigger family." My second point was: "I got a lot of great presents that I wanted, and I was able to share them with people who didn't have as many." Then my last point: "I wished that my father could be with me on Christmas, but at least he was safe." Then I closed with: "I learned that Christmas is what you make of it, and that made it great for me."

Just then, Miss Nelson walked back in the classroom.

"Okay, everyone, stop your work. I hope you're done. I want to introduce our new student now."

For a minute, I got so excited! I was about to gain a new friend. My heart was racing until I saw it was Alec from my neighborhood. He was the same boy who acted like a bully to my cousin, got beat up by his brother, and was mean to me.

No! I screamed on the inside.

He looked right at me and had the nerve to wave. I sank down in my seat. Of all the second grade classes at our school, why in the world did he have to be in mine? Just like the rest of the class was complaining about doing our work, I was upset about mean Alec being in our class. But I couldn't do anything about it. Oh, no!

• • • • •

After the whole week went by smoothly and we didn't have any problems, I thought, *Maybe I wasn't giving Alec a chance.*

Sure enough, Trey and the rest of the boys got along with us girls. At recess everything was going great. In every game everyone got picked, and everyone got to play. Alec seemed to act so much better when he was in school. He didn't cause any trouble. But he wasn't trying to be anybody's friend either.

At the same time, that didn't stop Trey from trying to get to know him. When Trey would try and sit next to Alec at lunch, Alec would take his tray and move somewhere else.

Miss Nelson would always give us time to help other kids when they needed it. One time Trey saw Alec not doing his work, so he went over and asked, "Do you want some help?"

Alec got smart and shot back, "Did I ask for your help?"

Yuck, it made me sick because Alec was not nice. But Trey didn't give up. At recess when Trey was team captain he picked Alec first for his team. But Alec said no and walked away to sit on the bench. Poor Trey was just trying to be a buddy, but Alec was trying not to hear that.

Brooke waited until Alec wasn't facing us and walked over to Trey. "That guy is so rude. Why are you trying so hard to be his friend?"

Trey defended himself by saying, "Didn't we say when we got back to school after break that we were going to be friends and get along?"

I wanted to say, *Trust me. It's better to not get along with him because Alec isn't the buddy-buddy type.* But why should I rock the boat and say something? Daddy always told me if something wasn't broken, don't fix it. I didn't really get what he meant, but I knew I didn't want Trey getting close to Alec. Since Alec didn't want that to happen either, there was no use in me saying anything about it.

When we got back into class, Miss Nelson said, "Class, I looked at your paragraphs from earlier this week, and most of you need to improve your writing skills. And you should be practicing your handwriting at home."

Trey yelled out, "But boys aren't supposed to write as pretty as girls, Miss Nelson."

"Trey, first raise your hand when you want to speak," she said to him. "And secondly, I don't buy that. Boys don't have to write pretty but your writing should be neat so that people can understand what you're trying to say. Particularly in my class there will be no excuses. Also, I'm speaking of the content and not just the handwriting. Your sentence points should help describe the main sentence."

Trey argued, "But—" And the class started laughing.

I saw Alec checking Trey out. He had a smirk on his face, and it bothered me. I couldn't tell if Alec liked the fact that Trey was acting like a class clown or not. Maybe he liked the way Trey spoke up. Either way, I just didn't want Alec in my class. He didn't need to know or like anything or anyone! I was going to keep my eye on him.

"This is the beginning of a new yea, and there's always something we can do better than the year before. That's why we make **resolutions**. Does anyone know what a resolution is?" Miss Nelson asked.

I thought I had the answer, but I decided not to say anything. Chanté quickly raised her hand.

"Yes, Chanté?"

"It's when you have the right answer."

"That's close but that's called a solution, not a resolution. Anyone else?" Another person got it wrong, and no one else wanted to try.

So Miss Nelson said, "Okay, a New Year's resolution is

when you make a goal to change something for the New Year. Your next assignment is to tell me what your New Year's resolution is. I'm asking you, class, how will you be a better person this year? What are your dreams?"

Alec spoke up, "This is stupid. We're only in the second grade. We don't have any dreams." But since he didn't say it loud enough for Miss Nelson to hear him, he didn't get in trouble. Yep, he was slick. The students around him started laughing, and Miss Nelson looked over to see what was going on.

"Class, I don't know what's funny, but this is work time. Start writing. Now!"

Everyone hurried to pick up their pencils and begin writing.

Once again, we had to write five sentences: one topic, three details, and one closing. We were all working really hard. I was wondering, *How am I going to be a better me and change?*

So this is what I wrote:

> I plan to be a wiser person this New Year. I will be wise and make my mom happy by cleaning my room. I will be wiser by thinking about other people's feelings. I will be much wiser and will keep learning all I can learn. This year I will make better choices and try to be a better girl.

Before I could read it over, the bell rang. We were told

to take our paragraphs and finish them for homework. I couldn't wait to read mine to Mommy.

We were getting ready to leave school and walk to the buses. Brooke, Chanté, Trey, and I were talking about our paragraphs. After a while I noticed Trey look back at Alec and turn around to talk with him.

Brooke called out to Trey for him to catch up with us.

"Come on, Trey. We're gonna miss the bus," she said.

I could tell something was going really wrong. Alec seemed to be paying attention to Trey lately. He was standing by the double doors to the gym and looked like he was up to something.

Trey didn't come any closer to us. He stood next to Alec and said loudly, "Um, I just wanna say I'm not going to be hanging out with you guys anymore."

I stopped in my tracks and asked him, "What are you saying?"

"You know, boys aren't supposed to hang out with girls like we're best buddies."

"You heard him," Alec said with a smirk.

Brooke walked back to Trey and asked, "Where is this coming from? We've hung out together since kindergarten."

"Well, we're not in kindergarten anymore. We're almost in the third grade."

"Right now you're in second," I told him. "And who told you not to hang out with girls? Was it Alec? You're not going to be our friend anymore because some new kid said so. Is that right? You've been trying to hang out with him all week, and he acted like he didn't want to. Why now?"

I already knew Alec was trouble, but I didn't let my friends know how bad he was. When Trey was trying so hard for Alec to like him, I had a feeling it would end up this way.

"Oh, Morgan, you're just being a drama queen," Trey said.

"A what?" I asked him.

Trey said, "That's what I hear them saying on TV when ladies make things bigger than what they are. Besides, girls make boys soft, and we just can't hang out anymore."

"Does that mean we're not friends either?" Brooke asked, as her eyes got watery.

I was more mad than sad that Trey didn't want to hang out with us anymore. Alec had put him up to telling us he couldn't be friends with us.

"Yeah. I guess that's what I'm saying. Deal with it," he said. Walking to the front door of the school, he tripped because he was trying to be all cool for Alec.

"But, Trey!" Brooke called out to him.

"Just let him go," I said to Brooke.

"But Alec is mean and rude, Morgan, and that's not good."

"Oh yeah, he is. But Trey is gonna have to see it for himself. What else can we do?"

"I don't know, but we have to do something. You and I care too much for people to not do anything."

"We already tried, Brooke." I gave her a hug and walked out the door.

When I got on the bus, it was just Alec and me. Trey wasn't around. Brooke wasn't there. And nobody else in our class was there. He smirked at me, but I didn't let him get to me. I turned the other way and looked out the window. The sky was dark just like my mood. I felt **dreary**.

● ● ● ● ●

When the new week started and Trey hadn't changed, Brooke kept trying to talk to him. She was really worried about him. It reminded me of when Trey was trying to be cool with Alec. Now she was trying to be friends with him again, and Trey kept ignoring her and making her feel worse.

I finally said, "Brooke, forget about those stupid boys. You, Chanté, and I can have our own crew."

"Okay," she said in a voice that didn't make me believe her.

When recess came, we were divided. It was boys against girls. And it took three days straight for them to beat us before we said we didn't wanna play with them anymore. I believed in my heart that if Miss Nelson knew what was going on, she wouldn't have it, but at recess she wasn't out there with us. She didn't know, and no one wanted to be a tattletale.

The week flew by, and it was Friday again. Miss Nelson stood in front of the class. "Today, class, we're going to learn about life science. Life science is a study of the different **organisms**—living things: plants, animals, even fungi are organisms."

Miss Nelson continued. "And one thing we're going to do is vote on a class pet."

"A hamster!" someone called out.

"Raise your hand, class."

"A snake!" Trey called out and Alec agreed.

"We definitely won't be getting a snake," Miss Nelson said.

"A baby chicken!"

"That's a nice idea, but remember to raise your hands."

"A frog," Brooke said. "Oops. I'm sorry, Miss Nelson. I was just so excited about a class pet that I forgot to raise my hand. Having a frog would be so fun."

"Yes, it will be fun provided you all are good. Also, we will study the stages of a tree. You see that big oak tree outside our window?" Everyone nodded. "Well, it's January, and we're going to study it from now until May to see how it changes."

Next she said, "We're also going to study fungi. They may not look like living organisms, but they are." Then Miss Nelson showed us a picture of a mushroom as an example.

"I know what those are. We eat those all the time at my house," Trey said.

"Today we're going to plant seeds and record in our

logbook how the seeds will change."

We were excited! But before we could plant any seeds, we had to pull out our science books from under our desks. We read that there were three things a plant needed to grow: water, food, and sunlight.

Then Miss Nelson passed around two seeds to everyone so that we could plant them and watch them grow.

"Class, we're going to plant one seed outside and one inside and see if they grow any differently," she said.

They were lima bean seeds. Yuck! I hated eating those things. But I guess it would be pretty cool to see how they grew. It looked kinda like a watermelon seed, but it wasn't black. It was white and had a circle shape on one side and pointy tip on the other.

"Now, I need you to make a **hypothesis**. A hypothesis is an educated guess of what you think will happen. Do you think the seeds will grow quicker on the inside or outside?"

"Outside," most of the class shouted. And I thought so too.

Then we all put on our coats and went outside. We each planted our seeds two inches apart. And because there were twenty-two of us in the class, there were two even rows. Miss Nelson was on one row helping us girls. The boys were on the other row acting like they didn't want our seeds touching theirs.

All of a sudden, we heard someone crying and yelling, "Ouch! Ouch! Ouch!"

Miss Nelson rushed over and we followed her to where the boys were working. Trey saw us coming and turned his back to us. He wouldn't even look at Miss Nelson.

"Trey! What's wrong? What happened? Turn around." I could tell that he didn't really want to, but he obeyed her. His right eye looked really swollen.

"Tell me right now what happened!" Miss Nelson demanded.

No one said anything. They acted like they didn't know, but I did. Alec had done something. You could look in his face and tell that he was up to some **mischief**. He was smiling and acting all proud of himself. He was supposed to be Trey's friend but anyone could tell he wasn't concerned about Trey at all.

Yep, I knew he'd done something awful. I was about to say something, but then I thought about him in the woods and his threat to me. To be honest, I was scared and chickened out.

"Trey, I insist that you tell me what happened to your eye. If you don't let me know, then we can't fix the problem. We're trying to plant seeds, and someone gets a black eye because they're playing around. Or, was this **intentional**?"

After Trey stopped crying, he said, "No, Miss Nelson. It was an accident. I don't know who I bumped into but my eye really hurts."

"Hurry and plant those beans, class," she said to the rest of us, as she took Trey inside.

I saw Alec look at Trey and punch his fist in his hands to keep him quiet. Sure enough, I was right. And Trey didn't say anything. I couldn't believe this. But then, I didn't say anything either.

Five minutes later, Miss Nelson came back outside with us and said, "Okay, I guess it was an accident. He can't even remember who he bumped into. Let's go back in and plant the inside beans."

At the end of the day, I went to Trey and said, "Are you sure you don't remember what happened? You have to know what happened. I know Alec hit you."

"Leave it alone, Morgan. Just drop it."

"You can't let people just hit you and you don't say anything," I tried to explain to him.

"I don't need any girl to tell me what to do. You think you're all that and know everything. Besides, if you're my friend, you should understand. You can't tell."

Letter to Dad

Dear Dad,

I think I hate school now. Don't get **paranoid** and be worried. I'm still a good student. It's just that mean people go to school, and it makes it hard on the nice people. I did make a New Year's **resolution** to be a wiser person. So I'll try not to be **dreary** and down and instead be positive.

Actually, I found out that I like science. We will be studying **organisms**. We may even get a class pet. What do you think we should get? But, not a snake, Dad. :-) I'm gonna make a **hypothesis** that we get a hamster. Most people in the class seem to want one. But if we don't stop with the **mischief**, we won't get any pet at all.

I plan to be a leader. So I have to be **intentional** and make it a point to tell everyone not to mess up. Sometimes that's not easy to do.

Your daughter,
Needing to be stronger, Morgan

Word Search

```
M O N C E U P O N A Y R
I P A R A N O I D O E O
S N G O L H D I L S T R
C K T S C Y A M O E O G
H C A E W P N L W C H A
I A T P N O U R I A Q N
E B N D A T O R R I D I
F I X T I H I H O T G S
S N P O F E M O J L N M
E R N Y L S W P N Z Z S
A S T A R I D R E A R Y
T E D H E S J U S T L H
```

DREARY

HYPOTHESIS

INTENTIONAL

MISCHIEF

ORGANISMS

PARANOID

RESOLUTIONS

Words to Know and Learn

1) par·a·noid (păr'ə-noid') *adjective*
Beinig unrealistically suspicious of others

2) res·o·lu·tions (rĕz'ə-lū'shəns) *noun*
Sincere promises to oneself to do something

3) drea·ry (drîr'ē) *adjective*
Dismal; bleak; boring; dull

4) or·gan·ism (ôr'gə-nĭz'əm) *noun*
A liviing thing, such as a plant, animal, or bacteria

5) hy·poth·e·sis (hī-pŏth'ĭ-sĭs) *noun*
A guess about something that can be tested

6) mis·chief (mĭs'chĭf) *noun*
Behavior that causes discomfort or annoyance in someone else

7) in·ten·tion·al (ĭn-tĕn'shə-nəl) *adjective*
Done on purpose; deliberate

Chapter 4

Following Me

"When are we going to get to the fun stuff? I'm sick and tired of recording 'no changes' for these lima beans," Alec complained.

"Me too!" Billy agreed. This boy was trying really hard to get on Alec's good side.

It was the middle of January and very cold. But Miss Nelson still made us go outside and write down our observations. The faster we did it, the faster we could come back inside. So I looked over at Brooke to see if she was doing her work, but she was looking mean like she had a problem with the assignment too.

When she noticed me looking at her, she came over to me and said, "Morgan, I'm tired of doing this too. Nothing is really growing."

"Don't follow them, Brooke. We have to take down what the plants are doing even if there is no change. We're different from the boys. We care about our grade. If they want to fail then let them."

"Yeah," Chanté said, as she eased her way into the conversation. "The boys don't have to do it if they don't want. Who cares about them anyway?"

Then I saw Alec snatch Trey's pencil out of his hand and throw it to the ground, saying, "What are you doing?"

"I'm writing down what I see changing in the lima beans," Trey answered back, as he bent down and picked up the pencil.

Alec reached over and grabbed Trey by his jacket collar. "I told you that I was sick and tired of looking at these beans and that means you should be tired too. If we all give up, then Miss Nelson won't make us do this dumb project anymore."

"Oh, okay," Trey said, **reluctantly** tossing his pencil back to the ground.

His eyes were almost watering. Miss Nelson had stepped inside for a few minutes, and I knew it wasn't going to be good leaving us outside with Alec. I was worried for my friends. I was worried for me.

"Everything was so much better when that mean boy wasn't here. He's hitting people. He's saying bad things. He's bullying people," Brooke said. "And he's only been here two weeks. I'm sick of him."

I wasn't trying to say "I told you so." But I looked over at Trey and he looked sad. He had left his friends because Alec said it wasn't good to hang out with us girls. I read in my Sunday school book that even in the Bible people had lessons to learn. I knew that meant I had to let Trey learn for himself too. But I didn't want to see anyone get a bad grade—friend or no friend.

Brooke tried again to talk to Trey but he wouldn't say anything to her. I could tell that it made her sad. I hugged her and told her, "It's okay, girl. Leave him alone."

Now that we were inside the classroom, we had to make **observations** about what we saw that was different from the seeds on the outside. Finally, there was a sprout— on an inside plant! Brooke saw it on hers first.

"Look! Look! I see a sprout coming!" she shouted. All of us girls rushed to see it. We were getting excited because we knew it would only be a little more time before the others started to grow.

Now we knew that seeds grew faster inside under a heat lamp than outside in forty-degree weather. But I didn't find that **ironic**.

"Class, I understand you're excited, but we have to keep it down. There are other classes on this floor who are studying," Miss Nelson reminded us. "At the end of the year we'll have Field Day, and you can yell all day long. But that day hasn't come yet, so calm down and take your seats."

When she turned toward the board, Trey walked over to Brooke and looked at her plant. "That's really—"

But before he could say anything else, Alec gave him a mean look like he was saying, *You're not supposed to be talking to her.* But that wasn't enough. He came over to Trey and brushed up hard against him. Then he said, "I'm gonna get you for that later on."

Trey didn't say anything. He was really scared, so he just turned the other way and looked down. Most of the time when Alec picked on a boy all the other boys laughed, but nobody was laughing now. This was not cool. Everybody knew Alec was scary. Right behind the teacher's back, he was way out of line and needed to be stopped.

"Okay, everyone, please sit down," Miss Nelson said again. "Now that we see a sprout on the inside and not on the outside, can anyone tell me what you are thinking so far?" she asked us.

"Lima beans grow faster on the inside than the outside. Duh," Alec said with a mocking voice.

"Okay. You're stating a fact from our observation, Alec. But what supports that fact?"

Then Alec didn't say anything. He just sat there looking like a dummy. And that's exactly how I felt about it. I'm not supposed to call anyone that name, but I couldn't help myself. He was getting on my nerves, and I was truly happy that he didn't have the answer. He wasn't a know-it-all, after all.

I quickly raised my hand. "Yes, Morgan? Do you know?"

"We're able to say that the sprout on the inside came up quicker than the outside because it's been getting the proper amount of water, soil, and sunlight. Not too much water, though, like when it rains outside. Also, it's been too cold outside so the sun wasn't shining on the plants like they needed it to." I smiled because I saw Miss Nelson nodding her head all the while I was speaking.

My teacher then said, "Very good, Morgan. Okay, class, we're going to take a few minutes to write paragraphs on what we saw today."

Again, I could hear Alec groaning.

Miss Nelson went right over to his desk. "Alec, is there a problem? I have heard you open your mouth too many times, and I've been letting you get away with it. Now that you've been here a couple weeks, you're not a new student anymore. And you need to know the rules. *I* run my class. I'm the only one who gets to make comments, and you do as I say. Is that clear?"

He didn't say anything. He looked toward the window and then back at her, but he didn't even answer Miss Nelson.

She bent down into his face and said, "I said, is that clear? I've talked to your dad before. Do I need to call him?"

Quickly, Alec opened his mouth and said, "No, ma'am. I understand."

Maybe I had **underestimated** Miss Nelson. Maybe she did know what was going on in her class. Of course she knew, because she was the only one who could make Alec straighten up like that. Finally!

● ● ● ● ●

The next day Alec was good in class; he didn't try Miss Nelson once. And he must have told the other boys to be good too, because they were raising their hands like never before.

They wanted to answer questions and stuff like the rest of us. We were learning how to round up numbers from 100 to 1,000 to the nearest hundreds place.

Miss Nelson was a great teacher. She explained every subject in a way that we could understand it. So she taught us a cool rule for rounding. If the number is 761, and if you're rounding to the nearest hundred, then you have to decide if it's 700 or 800. The trick is to look in the tens place and decide if you have to round up or down.

So the rule is: Find the number, look next door, and if it's five or more, add 1 more. We found the 7 and looked next door at the 6. Because it was 5 or more, we rounded up to 8. So, 761 rounded to the nearest hundred equals 800.

Then there's the number 549. You have to decide if it rounds to 500 or 600. Looking at the 4 in the tens place, it's less than 5 so you round down to 500. Then, like the number 999, some numbers are so close you know you round up, but using the rule, the second 9 is 5 or more so you round to 1,000.

"You students did a great lesson in rounding today. Tonight you have a worksheet to take home with twenty problems on it. I want you to do them all."

She seemed to ignore the sounds coming from the kids who didn't like math.

"Now let's go over cause and effect. This is a reading concept," Miss Nelson said to us.

I liked learning new things. She had written the definition on the board. *Cause* is one thing that makes another thing happen. Then right under that she had written: an *effect* is what happened from the cause.

Miss Nelson said, "We'll try one. Let's say Brooke left her science book at school, so she couldn't do her homework."

"Ooh!" a lot of kids started saying.

Brooke raised her hand. "Miss Nelson, why did you use me? I always do my homework."

"It's just an example, Brooke. I want you to tell me the answer. What is the cause and what is the effect?"

"Oh, okay," Brooke said in a happier voice. She was pleased the teacher didn't think she was a slacker. "The cause is: I left my book at school, and the effect is: I didn't get to do my homework."

"Correct. Trey, can you give me an example?"

"Yes, ma'am. Trey had a black eye, so he gave someone else a black eye." Trey said it in a tough, strong voice, looking right at Alec.

"No, Trey. That's not a good answer."

I could tell Miss Nelson wanted to know more about what Trey was talking about, but she didn't ask. He kept staring at Alec, and it was pretty tense for a moment. Brooke felt it and started coughing to break the silence.

I quickly raised my hand, and Miss Nelson called on me.

"Trey left his lunch money at home, so he couldn't buy his lunch today. The cause is: He left his lunch money, and the effect is: He couldn't get anything to eat."

"Very good, Morgan," Miss Nelson told me. She then called on Chanté.

"Okay. I studied for my spelling test, and I'm going to get an A. The cause is: I studied, and the effect is: I'm going to get an A. And I really will get an A because I studied hard for my test already, Miss Nelson," Chanté added quickly.

"Great, I know you can," our teacher said and smiled at her.

"Again, cause and effect is when something happens and it makes something else happen. So if you open up your reading books to page 45, you'll see the cause-and-effect sentences I want you to do. Remember though, the cause is not always in the front. For example, Alec was hungry because he skipped breakfast."

"I always eat my food!" Alec called out very loudly.

"Alec, it's just an example. Can you tell me the cause and effect in the sentence?"

"Yeah, the first thing you said about me not eating. Ugh . . . I don't know," Alec said, **frustrated**. It was like he wasn't even paying attention.

Quickly, I raised my hand. "Yes, Morgan?"

"The cause is: Alec skipped breakfast. And the effect is:

He was hungry."

"Very good. How about we take a little break now and go to recess. Okay?"

Everyone got excited. We put away our books, grabbed our jackets, and lined up at the back door. When Miss Nelson opened up the door, we all ran wild. That is, all of us except Alec. I could feel that he thought everyone was ganging up on him and not giving him any attention.

No one was on his side and he was alone. Maybe if he wasn't so mean in the beginning he could have a friend or two to lean on. Even the boys were tired of him, and they were making jokes about him.

"I guess the teacher thought he looked hungry. That's why she made up that sentence," Billy joked, rubbing his tummy to be funny.

It was like Alec had sonic hearing, and he wasn't going to take that. He walked clear across the playground and punched Billy in the stomach three times. And on the third time, Billy fell to the ground and started crying.

"I bet none of ya'll will make any jokes about me again. I run this class. And the next person who tries me will get more than a few hits in the stomach." Alec walked away, leaving all of us **stunned**.

An adult needed to know what was going on, but I was too scared to say anything. It was best I said nothing. The only thing to do was to just stay out of Alec London's way.

● ● ● ● ●

A month and a half later, something strange happened. All the inside lima beans had grown, except Alec's.

Miss Nelson studied his spot and couldn't figure out why his was the only one not growing. "Alec, did you even plant a bean?" He didn't give an answer. "Maybe your father knows if you planted a lima bean then."

"Yeah, yeah I did, Miss Nelson. Maybe somebody stole it."

"And who would steal your lima bean, Alec?"

The whole class knew he wasn't telling the truth because he kept telling us how stupid the whole thing was. Now he looked stupid being the only one without a sprout in the classroom.

"Class, this is a great example of reaping what you sow. If you don't plant anything, then nothing will grow. You have to plant your seeds, water them, and take care of them. Just like with your work. You can't learn something one day, not turn in your assignment for it, and then expect that you'll get a good grade if you do that. Alec, this is your third time not turning in your work."

"But somebody stole it!" Alec whined.

"Yes, that's what you said. But this is the third time, and I need to have a conference with your dad."

"No, no. I'll do the next one, I promise." He sounded like a big baby.

He was so tough before, but whenever she brought up his dad, he whined like a frightened little kid. Alec's threats to the class were getting worse. It seemed like we'd be okay as long as Miss Nelson had Alec's dad on call though.

At lunchtime, Brooke sat next to me. "I have to tell you something really important. This is bad."

Brooke was getting crazy with stuff lately. Nothing was ever bad but she made everything seem that way. One day she told me Miss Nelson was giving us a lot of homework to do, which wasn't bad. Then she said we weren't going to be able to go outside for recess because it rained, which really wasn't bad. I just looked at her and reached for my juice.

"Okay, Brooke," I told her. "What is it?"

"Morgan, I'm serious. It really is bad this time."

"Well, just tell me."

Brooke leaned in to my ear, like she had top secret info that no one else could hear. "Trey is getting ready to beat up Alec really bad."

Before she said that, I was getting up to throw away my trash. But hearing her secret, I almost dropped my tray on the floor. "What?"

"Yeah, and he said he's just waiting for Alec to mess with him again."

"Are you sure, Brooke?"

"That's exactly what he said. He's not going to take Alec's abuse anymore."

"Exactly what is he planning to do?" I asked.

"I'm not sure, but he sounds really serious to me. I'm not saying that Alec doesn't deserve to be hurt after he's hurt so many other people, but I just don't like the way

Trey was talking."

"Oh, my goodness," I said.

I wasn't too worried about what had gone on between Trey and Alec because Trey had told me to leave him alone. So that's what I did. He knew who he wanted to be friends with, but now things had gone very wrong. Over the past month, Alec roughed up too many people.

It was now the end of February, and I couldn't count how many people he had hurt. He had given Trey a black eye and a bruised arm. Since the first day Trey got on me for caring, I never said anything else or asked about how it happened anymore. No one had.

So I prayed, *Lord, I know bullying isn't right, and Alec is a pretty mean boy. I don't even like to ride the bus in the afternoons because I know him and his brother Antoine might do something stupid. That's why I sit right behind the bus driver so they can't mess with me. But Lord, Alec has messed with my friend, and I fear that something really bad will happen. What am I supposed to do? What do You want me to do? Help. Amen!*

I decided that I was going to talk Trey out of beating up Alec because he would get into trouble and could get suspended. As soon as I headed toward him, Brooke was right behind me. "What are you doing?"

"I'm going to talk him out if it."

"Well, if you're going to talk to him, then I'm going too," she said, following me.

"I'm sure you already said something when he first

told you. Right?"

"Yeah, but he doesn't listen to me."

"See. Then let me talk to him."

"But, Morgan, you need backup."

I waved my hand for her to go away, and then I sat next to Trey. "Can I talk to you for a minute?"

"I'm eating right now," Trey said, being very rude to me.

Then Brooke jumped in from the other side of the table and said, "She needs to talk to you now or the principal will later. I would talk to Morgan if I were you."

"You told her?" Trey said, as he stood up.

"Trey, what are you thinking? You know it will be nothing but trouble for you. Alec might hurt you bad," I said to him, standing up and gently pushing him back down.

"Or, I just might hurt him. He deserves it. I was thinking that I'm tired of Alec messing with me and everybody else. And I'm going to do something about it. You don't know what it feels like to be afraid to come to school. I know this is all my fault because I should've listened to you in the beginning, Morgan. You told me that Alec was a bad person. And I know it's gonna be a problem now because I'm not supposed to be talking to you guys. See, Alec is looking over here right now. I want him to try me outside though. I'll show him," Trey said, banging his fist on the table.

He was really fed up. I never heard Trey talk like that before. In fact, I never heard anyone talk like that. Now he was really scaring me, and something needed to be done.

"Does your mom know that Alec has been bullying you?"

"Just stay out of it, Morgan!"

It seemed like I couldn't stop Trey. He was **determined** not to be bullied anymore. When we went outside for recess, I watched him like a hawk. Every step he made, I followed close behind him. I couldn't let my friend get into any serious trouble, and there had to be something I could do to help. Then he saw me watching him.

"Morgan, what's going on?" he asked.

"I'm worried about you. What are you getting ready to do?"

"Stop worrying about me, stop caring. It's none of your business what I do. Whatever I have to do to get Alec off of me, that's what I'm going to do. So stop following me."

Letter to Dad

Dear Dad,

There was almost trouble on the playground at school today. **Reluctantly,** I'm writing you because I'm scared of what might happen tomorrow. The **observations** I'm making between my friend Trey and the bully Alec aren't good. Trey kept taking all Alec's meanness. But it looks like I **underestimated** Trey's toughness. Dad, he is so **frustrated** that he's ready to fight back. I'm **stunned** to be writing about this. It's really **ironic** that I care so much because Trey was acting mean to all us girls for a long time. But I do care, and I'm **determined** to do something good. I want to make you proud, Daddy. I love you so much.

Your daughter,
Ready to help, Morgan

Word Search

```
U  N  D  E  R  Y  U  R  T  H  R  H
E  S  T  I  M  A  T  E  D  U  E  O
C  M  M  C  L  C  O  D  E  T  L  M
A  F  A  E  I  A  S  G  T  D  U  E
B  R  V  N  B  T  L  E  E  C  C  S
I  A  O  I  S  K  E  N  R  A  T  W
N  R  T  D  L  I  N  J  M  P  A  E
I  G  L  O  O  U  O  F  I  C  N  E
T  E  N  S  T  A  H  L  N  O  T  T
F  R  U  S  T  R  A  T  E  D  L  H
B  U  N  G  A  L  O  W  D  X  Y  M
O  B  S  E  R  V  A  T  I  O  N  S
```

DETERMINED

FRUSTRATED

IRONIC

OBSERVATIONS

RELUCTANTLY

STUNNED

UNDERESTIMATED

(hint: "under" and "estimated" are apart)

Words to Know and Learn

1) **re·luc·tant·ly** (rĭ-lŭk'tənt lē) *adverb*
Unwilling; resistant; will not cooperate

2) **ob·ser·va·tions** (ŏb'zər-vā'shəns) *noun*
The acts of noting and recording something; making comments

3) **un·der·es·ti·mate** (ŭn'dər-ĕs'tə-māt') *verb*
Rate at too low a strength, value, or the like

4) **frus·trated** (frŭs'trāt' ed) *adjective*
Thwarted or disappointed at being thwarted

5) **stun** (stŭn) *verb*
Daze; shock

6) **i·ron·ic** (ī-rŏn'ĭk) also **i·ron·i·cal** (ī-rŏn'ĭ-kəl) *adjective*
Unexpected; opposite of the true meaning

7) **de·ter·mined** (dĭ-tûr'mĭnd) *adjective*
Being resolved to continue to work at something even when it is difficult

Chapter 5
Very Weak

The next day at recess, Trey and I were talking. I was still trying to talk him out of doing something he would be sorry about later. But Trey hadn't changed his mind. If anything, he was even more ready to teach Alec a lesson.

The next thing I knew, Alec was headed toward us. "I see you out here talking to this girl," Alec said to Trey. "You just don't listen, do you?"

Who did he think he was? In my mind, I was thinking, *Alec, you don't want to mess with Trey right now. You might wanna go back to where you were and leave Trey alone.*

I guess Alec could read what was on my face because he said, "I ain't scared of him."

Trey said, "You should be." Then he shoved Alec with so much force that Alec hit the ground. Trey didn't waste any time pounding the boy who had pushed him too hard too many times.

"Oh, no! There he goes!" This time Trey took the first punch. I knew it wasn't going to end well for him, so I dashed over to where Miss Nelson was sitting with a few other teachers. "Miss Nelson! Miss Nelson! You gotta come quick!"

"Morgan, slow down. What's wrong? I can't understand you when . . ."

I didn't even listen to what else she was saying. I just grabbed her by the arm and pulled her to where the boys were fighting on the basketball court. "It's Trey," I said, as we hurried in that direction.

When we reached the blacktop, I pointed to Trey and Alec. Even though Alec was on his feet, Trey was still getting the best of him. They were shoving each other, but Alec looked really weak. Just then we saw Trey knock Alec to the ground again.

Miss Nelson couldn't believe her eyes. She said in shock, "Oh my goodness!"

Then we heard Trey saying, "I'm tired of you picking on me, Alec. I'm sick of you telling me what to do. I'm tired of you making me think I'm no good. I ain't scared of you no more. Now, what you gon' do?" Trey kept shouting as he stood over Alec who was lying on the ground, twisting in pain.

Just as Trey lifted his foot and was about kick Alec in the side, Miss Nelson got in between them. "Stop it! Trey, what are you doing? This is totally **inappropriate** behavior. You are in big trouble, young man!"

I had never seen Trey so mad before. His eyes were red, and his face looked worse than any messed-up look that Alec ever had. And he wasn't backing down. I didn't want all of this bullying to come to this kind of end between Trey and Alec. I don't think anybody did. But with the teacher there or not, he'd had it with Alec. He just kept on kicking Alec and yelling at him.

Miss Nelson motioned for the other teachers to come over. One of the male teachers grabbed Trey and pulled him off of Alec. I was so glad when he did, before Trey really hurt him enough to be in the hospital.

Another teacher helped Alec get up off the ground. He was saying to Miss Nelson, "I didn't even do anything to him. He just jumped on me and knocked me down. I don't know why he just started kicking me all over. See, that's why I haven't been doing my work, Miss Nelson. I was scared of Trey. He told me I'd better do whatever he says."

Was he serious? I couldn't believe what I was hearing. Alec wasn't even close to telling the truth. He was so slick that he thought he could change the rules of the game. Alec was trying to make it seem like Trey was the bad guy all along, and that just wasn't true.

Miss Nelson just wrapped her arms around Alec to comfort him. "It's okay, son. Don't look at him while they **escort** him to the principal's office. The rest of you stay out here with Mr. Wade's class. I have to go to the office and report this."

When Alec walked off with Miss Nelson, he looked back at me and gave me a weak smile. He was hurt, but every time I tried to give him the benefit of the doubt, he made me regret it. I shook my head at him, letting him know he was wrong. He smiled a little wider and then turned back to the teacher.

Brooke and Chanté rushed up to me. Brooke opened her mouth before I could. "We have to do something."

Billy came over to where we were standing and said, "Alec just turned that all the way around on Trey. He whined to Miss Nelson and blamed Trey for the things he's been doing to us. Now Trey looks like the one who's guilty. Man, they might send him away."

"Oh, no. He's gonna go to jail, and he didn't even do anything wrong," Brooke said, broken up.

"I didn't think it would go this far, but I know if we don't help Trey, things could get a whole lot worse. Somebody needs to speak up," I told them.

Just then Mr. Wade called our class over to him. "The principal sent word that she's coming to your class to talk to you all today. You all should know that fighting at this school is unacceptable, young people. If you have any details or know anything about what brought this on, then it's time to speak up. Let's line up now so we can go inside."

"You know we can't say anything," Chanté said.

"Exactly. We can't tell anything because we know what Alec can do," agreed Billy.

This was horrible. I didn't just beat up anybody and would never do something like that, but at that moment I felt like Trey. So I had to stand up for what was right no matter what the cost. I also knew what Billy said was true. Alec's threats weren't fake; they were the real deal.

So I prayed, *Lord, please help me. Everything is happening so fast. I felt like I did the right thing when I got the teacher involved. What was I supposed to do, just let Trey hurt Alec badly and get into serious trouble? Lord, being a kid is hard, and I need Your help. Only You know what to do. I don't know what else to say except please help me find the words. In Jesus' name I pray. Amen.*

The entire class walked in silence because we all knew too much. The question was: Were we going to tell what we knew?

● ● ● ● ●

I had knots in my stomach because I was so worried. What had just happened on the playground scared me so badly. This was cause and effect all over again. Because Trey was scared to speak up, Alec pushed him around and acted like a bully. Because Alec was a bully, Trey couldn't take it anymore. Because Trey couldn't take it anymore, Trey jumped on Alec and beat him up.

Then, because Trey was getting ready to hurt Alec, I went to Miss Nelson. Because I went to Miss Nelson, the principal is coming to talk to our class. And if we didn't spill the beans, all of us were going to be in trouble. I didn't even wanna think about the effect of me getting in trouble at school.

Mr. Wade paged our teacher. Then he said to us, "Since Miss Nelson isn't back yet, I'll have to come back and check on your class until she gets here. But I still have to tend to my class. The office just sent me a message and said she'll be here soon. Until then, work on the math problems that are on the board. There will be absolutely no talking. This class already has enough explaining to do. Let's not add to it. Do you all understand?" he said firmly.

Rounds of "yes sir" went across the room.

I thought I had **mastered** rounding numbers 100 to 1,000 to the nearest hundred, but for some reason I couldn't even remember the rule. I was really worried. What was going on with Trey? Was he going to be suspended? Would they kick him out of school for good? Was Alec in the office telling more lies?

Billy sat behind me and whispered, "Okay, whatever the principal says—don't say anything. Remember, you don't know nothin'."

"Shhh!" Chanté said. "You're going to get us all in trouble."

Billy said, "We're going to be in worse trouble if we start **snitching** on Alec."

"We can handle it. Okay?" said Chanté.

I wasn't saying anything. My heart was just beating faster and faster like the time I got in trouble for pouring syrup on the kitchen floor at Mama's house because I wanted to see if I could slide in it. When Papa saw what I did, I thought I was gonna pass out, knowing I was in so much trouble.

Just let me do my work, I said to myself. *Problem #1, 614. The 6 is in the hundreds place, the 1 is in the tens, and the 4 is in the ones. Do I need to round 614 to 700 or round down to 600? Okay, when I look at the ones place . . . ugh! It has nothing to do with the ones place. Come on, Morgan, focus. Okay, because the 1 is under five it stays at 600. Problem #2, 962. The 6 is in the tens place and it's 5 or more so it rounds up to 1,000. Problem #3, 762. The 6 is in the tens place, and that is 5 or more, so it rounds up to 800. Problem #4, 251. It is a 5 so it rounds up to 300.*

I finished all the problems, and I was glad to be done.

The principal walked into our classroom with Miss Nelson, and neither one of them looked happy. My whole class was nervous and sank down in our seats. I felt like I had no words, and they hadn't begun to speak to us yet. This was serious.

Miss Nelson said, "I need everyone to put down their pencils and give their **undivided** attention to our principal, Dr. Sharpe."

I raised my hand.

"Yes, Morgan?"

"May I go and get some water?"

All the rest of the kids' hands in the classroom went up and "me too," echoed around the room.

"No, class. Everyone stay seated. We have to deal with this," Miss Nelson replied.

"But I have to go to the bathroom really bad," Billy said.

"What did your teacher say to you all?" Dr. Sharpe said. "I have some very angry parents in my office and two children who are in a lot of trouble. We need some answers to figure out just what happened. We're going to get to the bottom of this with your help. So let's be big boys and girls and have a serious conversation."

I got really nervous and sighed. I wished I was anywhere but here.

Dr. Sharpe spoke again, "Everybody here knows what happened. Two of your classmates got into a serious fight on the school's campus."

Billy called out, "We don't know anything about it, ma'am."

"Billy, please don't **interrupt** Dr. Sharpe," Miss Nelson said to him.

"Okay, all of you may not know what's going on, but I think there may be a few of you in here who can tell us more. I'm hearing two different versions of the story from those two young men."

"Oh, no! Do you think Trey is going to be kicked out of school?" Brooke whispered to me.

"I don't know, girl. Let's just wait. I hope not."

"Oh, Morgan, this is really not good." Brooke sounded very worried.

Dr. Sharpe said, "Class, I want you to be honest with me. You all play outside with both of these boys every day. Now, which one of you went and got Miss Nelson?" Everybody looked at me, so I slowly raised my hand. "Young lady, what is your name?"

"Morgan Love," I said in a low voice.

"Morgan, what made you go and get your teacher?"

I paused because I didn't wanna tell a fib to the principal. And I didn't wanna say anything to get anybody in trouble.

"Just talk to me. Tell me the truth about what happened," Dr. Sharpe said, as she walked near my desk.

"Well, Trey and Alec were arguing. And then Trey knocked Alec to the ground and started kicking him. I didn't want anyone to get hurt."

"So he had been bullying Alec? Is that right?"

I looked over at Billy and he had a worried look on his face. Then I looked at Dr. Sharpe and Miss Nelson. It might not be a good idea to tell on Alec, but no matter what, I had to help Trey and everybody else who was bullied by Alec. I had to tell the truth.

So I said, "No ma'am, Alec has been bullying most of the kids in this class since he got here. He even made the boys stop talking and playing with us girls. He's been hitting people and kicking people, especially Trey. And Trey finally got tired of it. We're all tired of it."

"Miss Nelson, did you know anything about this?"

"I most certainly did not, Dr. Sharpe," she said.

"She's never around when it happens," I told him.

"Do you leave your class unattended?" Dr. Sharpe asked our teacher in an unhappy voice.

Before she could answer, I said, "No, it's the times when we're walking outside to recess or whenever she turns her back. Alec is slick. He knows what he's doing. And he tells people he's gonna hurt us if we say anything. Trey was wrong but—"

Before I could say another word, Dr. Sharpe interrupted me and said, "That's all I needed to know, Morgan. You're saying Trey was fighting back, and that made it a good enough reason to start a fight. But you all have to think before you act. Fighting is not the answer. There are enough teachers at this school to go to and tell whenever you have a problem. Also, I'm always **available**."

Before leaving our room, the principal spoke quietly to Miss Nelson by the door. I felt relieved that I got all of that off of my chest. After our explaining session was over, we took a bathroom break. I went up to Billy, but he walked away from me.

When I went into the girls' bathroom, Chanté and Brooke turned their backs on me too. I had been there before, and I didn't wanna have that feeling of being alone again. But it didn't matter. I had opened my mouth to tell the truth, and my classmates were showing me that they didn't like me for it at all.

When we were getting ready to go home, Billy came up to me with a few of my classmates behind him and said,

"Thanks a lot. Now Alec is going to get us all because you opened your big mouth. Why did you have to be a hero and tell everything, Morgan?"

"I wasn't trying to be a hero. Dr. Sharpe asked me a question and I answered her. You all heard it."

"She didn't make you talk," Billy said.

"My parents taught me to tell the truth and to speak when spoken to."

"Well, my parents taught me not to be stupid and not to play with trouble. Alec is trouble, and Trey was trying to protect us," said Billy. "You're going to get us all messed up. Girls make me sick. You all are so dumb and very weak."

Letter to Dad

Dear Dad,

It was **inappropriate** for Trey to start a fight with Alec at school. He got an **escort** to the principal's office when they found out. The mean boy, Alec, has really **mastered** lying. Daddy, he twisted everything. I was the one that told the teacher on Alec. And some kids think that was **snitching**. The principal came to our class and we had to give her our **undivided** attention. She gave us a speech about being good and coming to her or another teacher if we get into trouble. We were all too scared to **interrupt** her. But she said she's **available** anytime to help us. I may need to go see her, Daddy, because since I told, my friends aren't happy.

> Your daughter,
> Stepped it up, Morgan

Word Search

```
E  S  P  M  C  A  R  C  E  S  I  N
T  S  H  L  A  K  A  Y  A  K  W  A
U  N  C  U  J  S  K  R  O  I  A  P
G  I  A  O  T  O  T  B  C  I  G  P
B  T  N  J  R  T  X  E  K  N  O  R
O  C  O  E  B  T  L  O  R  G  N  O
A  H  E  T  P  L  A  N  E  E  R  P
T  I  H  O  R  S  E  B  Z  F  D  R
U  N  D  I  V  I  D  E  D  Y  C  I
T  G  Z  E  L  B  A  L  I  A  V  A
O  R  B  I  N  T  E  R  R  U  P  T
T  R  A  N  S  P  O  R  T  Y  P  E
```

AVAILABLE

ESCORT

INAPPROPRIATE

(hint: find "appropriate" and connect "in")

INTERRUPT

MASTERED

SNITCHING

UNDIVIDED

Words to Know and Learn

1) in·ap·pro·pri·ate (ĭn'ə-prō'prē-ĭt) *adjective*
Unsuitable or improper

2) es·cort (ĕs'kôrt') *noun*
One or more persons accompanying another to guide or protect

3) mas·ter (măs'tər) *verb*
Develop a skill in or knowledge of something

4) snitch (snĭch) (Slang) *verb*
To tell a secret

5) undi·vid·ed (un-dĭ-vī'dĭd) *adjective*
Concentrated on one object, idea, etc.

6) in·ter·rupt (ĭn'tə-rŭpt') *verb*
Begin to speak before someone else has finished speaking

7) a·vail·a·ble (ə-vā'lə-bəl) *adjective*
Willing to serve or assist

Chapter 6

Strong Person

I stayed in my room all night and didn't even turn on my night light. The room was dark, and that's how I felt. My classmates thought I let them down completely.

Mom thought I wasn't feeling well and, actually, that was the truth. When she knocked on my door, I figured she was coming to check on me.

"Morgan, I need to talk to you, sweetie."

"I don't feel good, Mom." Placing the pillow over my head, I said, "Good night."

Because I wasn't allowed to lock any doors in the house, she came right on in and said, "Sweetheart, we need to talk."

I rolled over to the other side of the bed so I wouldn't have to face her. Just because she was talking and I had to listen didn't mean I had to like it. She started to rub my back, and I started crying.

"Oh, Morgan, come here," she said, feeling my pain.

I scooted over and put my head in her lap. "Oh, Mom! School is horrible, and nobody likes me. Can I go back to my old school?"

"You're not changing schools. It can't be that bad."

"Well, can I skip a grade after all? I don't wanna go back to that class."

"Not before the end of the school year, Morgan. If you're going to skip a grade, we'll have to look into that next year. You can't run away from your problems, baby. Okay?"

"But, Mommy, you don't understand. You don't know the full story," I told her.

"Actually, I do. I spoke with Miss Nelson."

I wiped my eyes. "You did?"

"Yes. They sent an e-mail to all of the parents about the kids in your class who were fighting at school. Miss Nelson also asked me to call her. As it turns out, my daughter was the hero of the day."

I was **chuckling** on the inside. There was no way I could be called a hero. I actually hated being me. Really, I was just trying to show that I cared and making sure nobody got hurt. But nobody cared about that. They thought I was just being a tattletale.

"It's honorable what you did, Morgan. You stopped a classmate from badly hurting another student and from getting into serious trouble. You don't need to feel bad because you stood up for what was right."

"But was it really right, Mom?"

"Morgan, how can you ask that? How would you feel if your friend ended up in the hospital?"

"That boy who was about to get hurt is not my friend."

"Was it the boy, Alec, from down the street?"

"Yes."

"What did he do?"

"He told a fib, Mom. He said that my friend Trey jumped on him for no reason and that's not true. He bullies everybody, and he's mean. Now, because I told on him everyone hates me."

"What do you mean, Morgan? But first, let me say this, I hope you didn't put yourself in the middle of that **nonsense**. I would never want you to risk your life or get hurt."

"No, when they started to argue and fight, I went and told the teacher. Then our principal came to our class to ask questions about what was going on."

Mom pulled me closer and rocked me back and forth in her arms. It had been a long time since she'd done that. Jayden was taking my place as her baby, but I wasn't jealous or anything. It was cool that I could share my mom with my little brother. It was like she was protecting me, telling me everything was going to be okay. And somehow, rocking back and forth in her arms, I could believe it. I could feel myself already getting stronger.

"Morgan, honey, I want you to listen to me and hear me clearly. It takes a really wise, smart, and tough person to stand up with **integrity**. Integrity means doing what's right. It means doing it even though you might have to stand alone and not care what others think. Like when you went and got the teacher in a time of danger. Trust me, something bad could have happened if you hadn't stepped in. Every parent in your grade is talking about this incident tonight. I am proud of you, pumpkin—very proud!"

I placed my head closer to her heart and she rocked me to sleep. Maybe I did do the right thing. It just sure didn't feel like I did.

• • • • •

I was so happy it was the weekend and I could be with my grandparents. They made me feel so much better. They were so silly. Chasing each other around the house and squirting each other with water guns helped me not to think about all of the drama at school.

It was almost Easter, and I wouldn't be surprised if they helped me search for Easter eggs. How fun that would be, but it probably wasn't going to happen. I just loved being around them, and they enjoyed my company too.

"All right, Morgan. You said you wanted to paint. Can you carry that can?" Papa asked me.

"No, sir," I said, trying to pick it up. It was so heavy.

"Well, grab those brushes. We have to paint this fence today or your grandma won't feed me," he said, making me laugh again.

There wasn't much prep work to be done. He had already stripped it down. All we had to do now was paint.

"So tell me what's been going on with you. How's

school and everything?" Papa asked me, as he showed me the best way to use the paintbrush.

Mama and Papa were good at checking on me to make sure I was doing okay. And that was all right with me. The truth was, a few weeks had gone by in school and none of the kids were speaking to me.

As it turned out, both Alec and Trey had gotten suspended. Trey, for starting the fight, and Alec, for all the things he'd done to everybody. They'd both be back in school on Monday though. I had butterflies in my stomach thinking about it and didn't know how I was going to face either of them.

"Can we just paint, Papa?"

"What! Morgan, you don't wanna talk to me? Those kids at school are giving you a hard time, huh?" I didn't answer. I just kept on making the fence look pretty. "You know, when I was your age there was this guy named Clyde. Clyde Jackson. He was about three inches taller than me and everywhere I went he was always two or three feet behind me, talking smack. You know what smack is?"

"Yes, sir," I said. "Smack is talking junk and teasing."

"Right. But listen now, I'm serious. He always had something to say about whatever I was doing. He'd call me all kinds of names. One day I was fed up with him. I stood in front of our whole class and gave him a piece of my mind. Clyde stood there just crying his eyes out. I had no idea why. Later, I found out he lived in a foster home and didn't have any parents. No family or nothing. Then I knew all the anger he showed to me was really because he didn't have things right in his own life."

"Really, Papa?" I said, wondering if it was a true story or he was just trying to teach me something.

"Yes, I told you I was serious. Pretty sad, huh? Needless to say, we became friends. My family started inviting him over to dinner and to stay overnight. We prayed for him and showed him some of the love he was missing. And, you know what? He changed. You guys are so young; you're only in elementary school, but y'all still feel stuff. Nowadays, who knows what some of those kids in your class are going through? I know it's hard not having your dad here but just stay strong, Morgan. Besides, look at who you do have on your side—your mom and stepdad, your baby brother, and us."

Papa always made sense. He pleasantly inspected the wood I'd repainted. "As many perfect strokes as I've done, you've done twice as many. You can do anything you put your mind to. That means weather the storm with the crazy things going on in your class too. It'll all work out in the end."

"Weather the storm? What does that mean?" I asked.

"It means ride it out. The tide is high. You know, like in the story about the fishermen?"

"No."

"You mean, you've never heard the story about Jesus and the fishermen on the boat?"

"No, sir."

"Sara, come on out here and tell this child the story about the fishermen and Jesus on the boat."

"I'd love too. Y'all need to take a break, anyway," Mama said, as she came outside with carrot cake and milk.

"Oh, it's one of my favorite stories. See, the **disciples** and Jesus were on a boat and a storm came. The disciples got scared because the boat was rocking and the sky was thundering. They just knew that the boat was going to sink. And Jesus was asleep at the back of the boat. So they went and woke Him up for help. Jesus got up and told the water, 'Hush, be still.' Then when the wind stopped blowing so hard, everything was okay. But He asked His disciples, 'Why are you afraid? Do you still have no faith?' See, I just love that story. It comes from the book of Mark in chapter 4."

"Why do you love it, Mama?" I asked, with my mouth full of cake. As I waited for her answer, I reached for my milk and took a big gulp. Then I ate another big bite of my cake. And one more sip of milk. It was all good.

"Are you ready?" Mama asked.

"Yes, ma'am."

"What do you think the moral of the story is that I just told to you, Morgan?"

"That God is with us all the time, and we don't have to worry?"

"Yes, that's exactly right. Even when you think He's asleep or when the waters are **raging** or when times are really tough. God's got you, and He's going to make everything okay. You can make it if you have faith and stay strong."

"What a great story," I said, as I finished my dessert. "And what a great slice of cake. Mama, you sure can bake."

"Yeah, baby, I can," she said as she winked.

I sure had a great time at my grandparents' house.

• • • • •

Back at home, Daddy Derek asked me to play with him outside. I guess Mom had told him that I wanted to spend some time with him. I looked out and saw Antoine and Alec outside playing some game, and I had no **intention** of going anywhere near them.

"That's okay. I'm fine. You can go and help Mom or play with the baby. I'm just going to read a book or something," I told him.

"Morgan, I saw you reading yesterday and the two days before that. Let's go outside and get some fresh air. Spring is here. Come on, just you and me."

He didn't tell me to get up and go outside like it was an order or something, but he wasn't taking no for an answer either. Slowly, I got off the couch. I put on my jacket and headed toward the front door.

"No, you don't have to go out the front door. Come to the garage so you can help me with something."

I went downstairs to the garage door and opened it. Daddy Derek was right behind me. "Why don't you turn to the left and go over by the carport. I need you to test something out for me and make sure it works okay."

Just as I turned to the left, I saw a beautiful pink bicycle with pink and white streamers hanging from the handlebars. "Wow!" I screamed. "What's this for?"

"For me having the best daughter a father could have. You've been doing such an excellent job at school. I know things have been tough for you, and we haven't had a chance to talk about it. I'm so proud of you, and I knew your old bicycle was getting too small. Your mom and I finally decided on this shiny new one."

"Do you like it, Morgan?" Mommy asked, as she came outside with Jayden. He was getting so big.

"Go ahead and try it out," Daddy Derek said.

"Okay! I got a new bike," I squealed, as I jumped on it to ride.

As I took off flying down the driveway, the streamers on my handlebars were blowing in the breeze. Then right before I touched the street, Antoine and Alec rode by on their scooters. I whipped that bike around so fast and went right back into the garage.

"It rides great. Thank you so much."

Daddy Derek said with surprise, "You didn't even ride it long enough to get a good feel for it. Go on. Ride it some more."

"I'm going to try it a little later when the sun goes down. It's too hot right now."

"It's only about 70 degrees, Morgan. It's a pretty day," Mom said.

"What's going on?" Daddy Derek said. He was looking

right at the boys who weren't looking too nice at me.

"Come on, Morgan. We're going to fix this right now," Mom said, as she placed the baby in the stroller.

"What do you mean, come on?" I said, more frightened than if I was in a very bad thunderstorm or lost in the woods, unable to find my way home.

"We're gonna go and talk to their parents. We aren't going to let these boys make you feel uncomfortable in your own neighborhood."

"I'll take her. I talked with Mr. London once or twice and he seems like a nice guy," Daddy Derek said.

"Honey, you think that's a good idea?" she asked.

He gave Mom a kiss on the cheek. "We'll be fine. We'll be right back."

The last thing I wanted to do was go over to the Londons' home. I'm not sure if adults can talk about things like us kids can. You could see worry all over my face, but unfortunately, my feet were on the move.

"Don't worry about it, baby," Daddy Derek said, feeling my fear.

Before we got to the door, Alec and Antoine pulled into their driveway. "Y'all need something?" Antoine called out.

"Good afternoon, young man. Is your dad home?"

"He don't wanna talk to anybody. He's watching basketball and don't wanna be bothered. That's why he kicked us out."

"Would you tell him I'm here, or do you need me to ring the doorbell?"

"I'll go tell him," Antoine said and went inside.

Alec didn't say anything to me, and I liked it that way. But he didn't stay around for us to talk to his dad either. He ran to the back of the house to get out of sight. When he was away from us, I felt a little better. That is, until the front door opened.

"You wanted to talk to me, man? What's up?" Mr. London said in a not-so-nice voice.

"Is everything okay?" Daddy Derek asked.

"It was until you interrupted my game. What you want?"

"Well, I wanted to talk to you about your boys."

"Did they go over there bothering you all again? I told them to stay away and mind their own business."

"No, no. My daughter . . . "

"Uh huh. I know about your daughter. She's the one who got my son in trouble."

"No, she didn't get your boy in trouble. She just told the truth like she was supposed to."

"Wait a minute. What is this about? You're coming over here talking about my sons and stuff."

"You need to know that your sons are **intimidating** other kids. Morgan is afraid to go out into her own neighborhood because of them."

"Then you need to toughen her up."

Mr. London came out of his front door and got real close to Daddy Derek's face. He said in a threatening way, "Look, I don't know who you think you're dealing with, but I don't play. I don't play with nobody all up in my business—so you'd better back down. I don't take no stuff off of nobody because I'm a strong person."

Letter to Dad

Dear Dad,

This is not a chuckling matter. Daddy Derek had it with me being bothered by the nonsense Alec and his brother were doing to make me scared. Remember when I told you that I had to tell the teacher on Trey? Well, although I had integrity and told the truth, folks are still mad at me. I'm trying to have faith because Mama told me the story of the disciples in the boat. The waters were raging and they learned to have faith and trust the Lord. Daddy Derek had good intentions when he tried to fix everything with the London boys, but that probably wasn't a good idea. See, Mr. London is even more intimidating than his sons. We're in a pickle.

Your daughter,
Shaking in my shoes, Morgan

Word Search

```
G  I  G  G  L  E  R  Z  J  D  L  T
N  N  O  N  S  E  N  S  E  T  O  S
I  T  L  T  H  R  E  E  I  S  U  N
T  I  D  S  R  A  E  B  N  E  T  O
A  M  I  D  A  Y  Z  O  T  L  T  I
D  I  L  F  V  J  I  H  E  P  O  T
I  D  O  Z  L  T  Q  X  G  I  L  N
M  A  C  G  N  I  G  A  R  C  U  E
I  T  K  E  S  C  T  G  I  S  N  T
S  I  T  X  U  K  W  L  T  I  C  N
N  N  P  A  N  E  N  A  Y  D  H  I
I  G  N  I  L  K  C  U  H  C  G  O
```

CHUCKLING

DISCIPLES

INTEGRITY

INTENTIONS

INTIMIDATING

NONSENSE

RAGING

Words to Know and Learn

1) chuck·le (chŭk'əl) *verb*
To laugh quietly with mild amusement or satisfaction

2) non·sense (nŏn'sĕns', –səns) *noun*
Behavior or language that is foolish or absurd

3) in·teg·ri·ty (ĭn–tĕg'rĭ–tē) *noun*
Strong sense of honesty; firm moral character

4) dis·ci·ple (dĭ–sī'pəl) *noun*
One of the original followers of Jesus

5) rag·ing (rā'jĭng) *adjective*
Wild, violent

6) in·ten·tion (ĭn–tĕn'shən) *noun*
A course of action that one intends to follow

7) in·tim·i·date (ĭn–tĭm'ĭ–dāt') *verb*
To make timid; fill with fear

Chapter 7

Little Girl

I stood there shaking at Mr. London's door. His eyes were red, and he was making his hand into a fist. It was like he wanted to hurt Daddy Derek and for no reason. We came over here to have a calm conversation about his sons, and Mr. London was getting loud. I didn't know what to do—so I just prayed.

Lord, I know his sons are mean, and this guy is their dad, so if they are like him, there's no telling what he could do. We need You. We need You right now to help us, in Jesus' name. Amen.

Daddy Derek must have been reading my mind because he said, "London, look man. I've been praying about this thing, and I didn't plan to come over here and get you upset. Can we talk?"

"Yeah, man. We can talk. Tell me something I don't

know," Mr. London said, backing up out of Daddy Derek's face.

"Morgan, sweetie, why don't you go on home. Practice on that bike some more," said Daddy Derek.

I looked up at him as if to ask him, *Are you sure?* When really, home is where I wanted to be. At the same time, I didn't wanna leave him, but I had to have faith that everything would be okay. They were adults and could handle it. Well, I hoped so. Plus, I'd talked to Jesus, and I knew He could keep the peace.

"Go ahead," Daddy Derek told me when I wasn't moving fast enough.

As soon as he saw me riding away, he walked inside with Mr. London. I rode down to my house and then back to the Londons' house. Then I rode back down to my house and up to their house again. I kept going back and forth because it was like I had to keep watch over Daddy Derek. I didn't wanna be the one to tell Mom and make her worry, but I knew I needed to stay nearby.

After almost an hour had passed, I was tired of riding my bike. I stopped in front of our house and Mom came out to call me inside.

"Morgan, where's your dad?"

"He's down at Mr. London's house."

"Okay, come on in and wash up so you can eat."

"Should I go down there and get him?" I asked.

"No, honey. Your dad will take care of this problem. He'll be home soon."

If she knew what I knew she wouldn't want him to stay down there too long. The London guys were scary. What if they were down there beating him up in the basement? Or what if they had him tied up and locked away in a room? Or worse.

But I didn't wanna think about the worst. I kept saying to myself that he was going to be okay. Having faith wasn't easy, but I had to stop worrying and trust God.

I was almost done with dinner, and too much time had passed. Just as I was about to pull Mom up so that we could go and get Daddy Derek, the top lock on the front door clicked open. I jumped up from the table and ran into his arms.

"What's wrong, Morgan?" he said, hugging me back. "I'm so glad you care about me. I'm okay."

"Yes, you're okay!" I said excitedly.

"Now, what's going on?" Mommy asked, as she held baby Jayden. "Why is Morgan so **stressed**? She acts like she hasn't seen you in months."

"The Londons are a bit of an unhappy group. They have a lot of anger in that house, and Morgan **witnessed** some of it."

"What?" Mom said.

"She was always safe. I sent her home and went inside to talk to him. So now I've got great news. Today Mr. London prayed to receive Christ. I won't go into the details, but he's been struggling for a long time. It's all going to change now because he opened his heart to God, and because he did, it's going to make a difference in those boys."

"You think so? You think they won't be bad anymore?" I asked.

"There's a good chance, pumpkin. God can do amazing things. He knows us so well, even down to the strands of hair on our heads. I know it was a divine appointment that He sent me over to their house today. And I don't want you to worry. You're too young for that. You just have to learn to trust God more."

"I did pray for them," I told them.

Daddy Derek said, "And look at how God answered your prayer."

"How do you know he wasn't faking?" I asked.

"Well, Morgan, you never know what's in a person's heart. I just tell them the Word and share the gospel. Then it's up to those who hear it to be honest about what they do with it. But Mr. London's tears seemed real. I do know that. I'm going to be **counseling** him to help him grow in his faith. Once God is in our heart, there's still work to be done in order for us to walk with Him. We're all growing."

That night before I went to sleep, I got on my knees and prayed, *Lord, thank You for doing more than I asked. I just wanted Daddy Derek to be okay, but You made Mr. London be okay too. Help me to trust You more. I love You, Lord. Now I know that having faith pays off.*

• • • • •

"Miss Nelson?" Billy asked. "I thought we were getting a class pet."

"You were supposed to get a class pet. But with everything that took place this semester, the idea of a class pet went out the window. I thought you all understood that. Since you guys can't get along, and you have trouble telling the truth, we'll just have to learn science another way."

"Aw man," Billy groaned.

"Speaking of science, I have something to show you. Class, let's line up to go outside."

For the past few weeks, I had been standing at the front of the line, closest to the teacher. I was trying to stay away from all of my "not so friendly" friends. Everybody was still mad at me, so I thought it would be best to stay near Miss Nelson.

When Trey came back to school, he wasn't talking to anybody. Alec came back, and he wasn't talking to anybody either. Brooke and Chanté hung out more because I was out of the picture, and they didn't play with anybody else. Billy tried to talk to everybody, but because he was so annoying, nobody wanted to talk to him. Everyone pretty much stayed to themselves.

Recess was so dull and boring, but we all wanted to know what Miss Nelson wanted to show us. As we walked closer to the fence behind the swings, our eyes grew extra big. There were two rows of full-grown lima beans!

"Hey! Our experiment worked!" Billy shouted.

"That's right. Given enough time and under the right

conditions, nature found a way for our seeds to sprout. Because they weren't contained in small cups, they had room to grow. Now we have a full crop of them. Class, take a few minutes to make some observations, and then we'll go inside to write our paper."

Brooke and Chanté walked over to me. "Hey, can we talk to you?" Brooke said.

"Yeah, Miss Nelson didn't say we couldn't talk," I said back.

"We miss you, Morgan," Chanté blurted out. "We were wrong by not talking to you this whole time."

"Yeah. I guess I didn't want Trey to get in trouble, and you told on him. I don't know," Brooke said, sounding confused.

"It's okay," I said. "I know he's your buddy."

"He was my buddy," Brooke said, looking over at Trey who was writing his notes.

"He'll come around," I said.

"So, do you forgive us?" Chanté asked.

I shrugged my shoulders. I knew I was supposed to forgive them, but it was hard. Brooke and I had already been through this once, and then she turned against me again. I was supposed to say that it was okay and just move on. But I didn't know if I could.

"Five more minutes, class. I see a lot of talking going on. Now, it's fine to compare notes, but you need to make your own observations," Miss Nelson reminded us.

"Hey, Morgan," Trey called from behind.

I turned to face him. "Yeah?"

"Uh, I just wanna tell you, um, um . . . I don't know . . . you're a real cool girl."

"What? I got you in trouble. What makes you say that?"

"I've just been thinking about it. I was so mad at Alec, and I could've hurt him if you didn't get the teacher to step in. I don't know what would've happened."

Then Trey reached out his hand for me to shake it. I smiled and extended mine back. As soon as I turned around, I bumped straight into Alec. I just took a real deep breath before I said anything.

"Sorry," I said, letting him know that I didn't want any trouble.

"No, it's cool. Look, your dad came to my house and um, um," he started. Then he just stood there for a minute.

I guess he couldn't find the right words to say. His face started looking worried. I was confused.

"Just say it."

Alec spouted, "My dad lost his job. That's why we had to move into your neighborhood."

"Wait. What did his job and our neighborhood have to do with anything?"

"Our old house was twice the size of the one we have now. But since my dad lost his job, he said we had to **down-size** because we're only living on my mom's salary. He's been mean and doing a lot of stuff he didn't used to do before. And I guess it made me and my brother angry, so we took it out on other people. Thanks to your daddy coming over, our house is calmer now. Things are much better. Our dad even told us he's sorry for how he's been treating us. I didn't deserve you helping me, Morgan, but I'm glad you did. I guess girls are good for something after all."

We laughed a little, and it was time for us to go back to class. I know I was supposed to write a paper about the lima beans experiment, but all I could do was write one about how my friends had grown and changed.

It was just like how the lima beans outside went through different temperature changes and weather conditions but finally sprouted the way we wanted them to. Even though in the beginning it took a while due to the cold. My friends did the same thing, sort of. It took everyone some time to come around to know that my heart was in the right place all along.

As far as Alec goes, maybe we could be buddies too. Naw! That was a stretch. But it's good to know that he won't be **terrorizing** anybody anymore.

• • • • •

I didn't really think I wanted to be best buddies with Brooke and Chanté anymore. But I guess since I couldn't stop thinking about them, that means I really did want them to be my friends.

When I got home from staying overnight at Mama and Papa's house, I was surprised to see the tea set on the table. Oh, wow, tea time! It was one of my most favorite things to do with Mommy.

"Go on and get changed. I put a nice dress on your bed for you," my mom said.

"What's going on? Aren't we going to have mommy and daughter tea time?"

"We sure are."

"Wait. Then why are there six places?" I asked, as I counted the cups.

"You're going to ruin the surprise. Now, go and get dressed."

I hurried because the **anticipation** had me excited. I quickly slipped into my pink and yellow dress and ran downstairs to the sound of the doorbell. As I peeked through the glass door, I saw Chanté.

"Hey, Morgan! Thanks for inviting me. This is my mom, Mrs. West."

"Hello! Come on in. Nice to meet you," I said to her mom.

Chanté didn't look anything like her mom. She was tall and her mom was much shorter than my mom.

Before I could close the door, I saw two more people walking up the stairs to the house. It was Brooke and her mother. To my surprise, they looked like twins! I didn't know two people could look so much alike. On top of that, they could be models. Brooke's hair was down, and I'd never seen her wear it that way. She looked really pretty.

"Hi, Morgan! Here are some muffins to have with our tea. Thanks for inviting me over," Brooke said.

Who said I invited you over? I thought. The way they had

treated me was mean and plain wrong, especially Brooke. If it was up to me, no one would be here but Mommy and me. I knew this was all her doing. Man, now we had to talk and make up and be buddies again. I couldn't wait for them to leave.

When I didn't say anything to her, Brooke just looked at me as I looked at her.

Then Mommy came to my rescue. "Ladies, why don't y'all come on in," she said.

I didn't even know that she knew their moms. As the three of us sat down at the table, we noticed our mothers were talking and laughing like the best of friends.

"You girls won't believe this," Mom said, as she took her seat. "We're all sorority sisters of Beta Gamma Pi. We were talking at a meeting last month and realized our daughters were in the same class. Isn't that something?"

"Yes, I'd say it is. Since my daughter's been sitting at home pouting about losing her best girlfriend, we thought we'd get you all together. We want to talk to you about what friendship is all about," said Brooke's mom.

Chanté's mom spoke next. "A few months ago, my daughter was so excited that she had made some new friends. Then, all of a sudden, she wasn't all smiles anymore. It was good for everyone when you all got along. Chanté, I first wanna say to you that you were so happy to be friends with Morgan. Then she worked it out so the three of you guys could hang out together. But when one person got upset with her, you did the same thing, and not

116

for your own reasons. You went along with the class. Well, a true friend sticks up for her buddy even if the two have to stand together. If that's your girl, and she's doing what's right, then you should help her. Do you understand?"

"Yes, ma'am. And I told Morgan how bad I felt. I didn't wanna hang out with Brooke or anybody because I knew I'd done the wrong thing by telling Morgan I didn't wanna be her friend anymore," Chanté said, as she started to cry.

"Girls, we don't want you to cry. Okay? We just want you to learn right from wrong. And if we don't tell you how to be good friends, then you'll just keep making the same mistakes."

Chanté fell into her mother's arms.

Then it was Brooke's mom's turn again. "I've got three kids at home." Then she spoke to her daughter. "Brooke, I was so excited that you had a friend. All I recall hearing was 'Morgan this and Morgan that.' Then right before Thanksgiving, you all fell out. After that, you were so excited when you became friends again. So, the beginning of the year started off with a blast—a new year and a new start. But then you got mad with Morgan again, Brooke." Her mom surprised me. She knew the whole story.

"I just didn't think she was supposed to tell," Brooke said in a low voice.

"Your friend Trey did something wrong. He didn't handle the situation correctly. If someone was bullying him, he should have talked to an adult about it. Instead, he tried to handle it his way by starting a fight. Why shouldn't

Morgan tell something like that to keep someone from getting badly hurt?"

"I know now that she did the right thing. Even Trey told her she did," Brooke said.

"He did?" Mom asked, looking at me.

"Yes, ma'am. He said he was glad that I stopped him before he hurt somebody."

"At first I didn't think about it that way," Brooke admitted.

"See, girls, just because you don't agree with your friends doesn't mean you have to stop being friends with them. You're supposed to be able to talk things out and pray about things. And because you all are so young, talk to your parents so you can get some **clarity** about what's right and what's wrong. Friends shouldn't pressure friends to follow their lead. That's another form of bullying and that's not right either," said Brooke's mom.

Then Brooke started crying. "I told her I was sorry. I don't think she's going to forgive me this time."

Then it was Mommy's turn to speak. "And that's what brings me to my point. Morgan, in this life we're not going to be perfect. We can try our hardest to be, but we will never be perfect. Little ladies, give each other grace. The Bible tells us we're supposed to forgive seventy times seven. That means keep on forgiving."

Mommy turned to me and asked, "And how many times has Brooke done something to you for you to forgive her?"

"Twice."

"Well, you've got a whole bunch more times to forgive her. You ladies have to value your friendships. Enough said? Now, we're going to have our tea in the dining room. The three of you can sit in here and talk."

Our moms got up and left us alone to talk. We looked at each other, laughed, and hugged. Then we went into the other room with our moms and enjoyed our tea and snacks. I was happy to have my friends back the way we used to be.

We were where we should be: young girls growing into young ladies, changing every day. We're learning that girls can do anything we put our mind to do—we can even stand up for what's right!

It was a good day. And it got even better when the mailman came and I got a letter from my dad. I ripped open the envelope and read it. His letter was short, but sweet.

Hey Morgan!

It's your dad! I miss you, and I love you. Your letters mean the world to me, so keep them coming. We can't do the video conference right now because we're sailing the high seas and don't get much of a signal out here. But I want you to know I'm proud of you, Morgan. Not many people can stand up and do what's right at your age. My young lady can. Keep on being awesome.

Love,

Your Daddy

P.S. I'm proud of you! That's my growing-up little girl.

Letter to Dad

Dear Dad,

I got your letter! I got your letter! Now I'm not **stressed** and wondering if you're okay. I know you're okay. I have friends again, and they **witnessed** how happy I was when I opened your letter. We had a tea party, and our moms were **counseling** us on how to be great friends.

Oh yeah, I found out why Alec was being so mean. His family had to **downsize** because his dad lost his job, and the tension came from that. Hopefully, he won't be **terrorizing** anyone else anymore.

But forget all of that. I miss you, Dad, and the **anticipation** of seeing you is getting to me. Please give me some **clarity** on when I'll see you again.

Your daughter,

Speaking up, Morgan

Word Search

```
S  D  E  S  S  E  N  T  I  W  D  O
A  N  T  I  C  I  P  A  T  I  O  N
S  E  A  R  C  H  I  N  G  C  W  X
F  S  C  O  U  N  S  E  L  I  N  G
O  T  S  P  E  A  K  A  U  P  S  R
R  R  C  F  E  A  R  N  O  T  I  E
W  E  N  H  E  I  S  N  O  W  Z  S
O  S  E  I  T  D  A  R  C  Y  E  O
R  S  T  Y  T  I  R  A  L  C  F  L
D  E  N  I  N  T  H  G  I  E  N  V
S  D  I  S  F  U  N  S  E  V  E  E
T  E  R  R  O  R  I  Z  I  N  G  D
```

ANTICIPATION

CLARITY

COUNSELING

DOWNSIZE

STRESSED

TERRORIZING

WITNESSED

Words to Know and Learn

1) stress (strĕs) *noun*
Physical or mental pressure

2) wit·ness (wĭt'nĭs) *verb*
To watch or be present at

3) coun·sel (koun'səl) *noun*
Advice or guidance given by a person who knows the subject well

4) down·size (doun'sīz') *verb*
To reduce in number or size

5) ter·ror·ize (tĕr'ə-rīz') *verb*
To fill or overpower with terror; to make afraid

6) an·tic·i·pa·tion (ăn-tĭs'ə-pā'shən) *noun*
An expectation

7) clar·i·ty (klăr'ĭ-tē) *noun*
A clear idea

1. Morgan Love wants to spend time with her stepdad, but her new cousin Drake wants time with him alone. Do you think Morgan should tell Daddy Derek that she feels left out? When you are frustrated with a situation at home, do you tell your parents how you feel?

2. When Morgan opens all her presents, she brags on how nice they are. Then she notices her cousins are sad. Do you believe Morgan should keep talking about her presents when her cousins don't have as much as she does? Is it ever nice to brag?

3. Morgan does not like that Alec, a boy from her neighborhood, is in her class. If Alec is mean at home, do you think that he will be mean at school? When is it best to give people another chance?

4. Alec is bullying kids in the class, and Morgan wants to tell. Why do her friends want her not to tell? Do you think telling adults when your class-mates do something wrong is a good idea?

5. Instead of talking over his problem with his parents or a teacher at school, Trey tries to handle the boy who bullies him by fighting back.

Do you think that Morgan should have told the teacher to stop the fight before someone got hurt? Do you feel it is wrong that Morgan's friends were mad at her for speaking up? What are ways you can make sure you help your friends understand what is right and wrong?

6. Morgan's mom lifts her spirits and tells her that she does not need to be afraid to go to school. Morgan then found out that bullies are people who have bigger issues and take their problems out on other people. What was Alec's bigger issue? Do you feel God expects you to take the time to understand why people act the way that they do?

7. Finally at school all of Morgan's friends came around. The girls agreed that Morgan should have told, and the boys thanked her for helping them not make a bigger mistake. Do you think they all were right to thank Morgan? Have you ever needed to thank a friend who helped you get out of trouble?

I want to write a letter to:

Dear

Words are fun to learn.
Words I would like to learn are:

_____

_____

_____

_____

_____

_____

_____

_____

_____

_____

_____

_____

_____

_____

_____

_____

_____

_____

Worksheet 1

Rounding: Round the following numbers to the nearest hundred.

Instructions: To round to the nearest hundred, look in the tens place. If the digit is 5 or more, round the number up. If the digit in the tens place is 4 or less, round the number down.

Example: 654 is rounded to 700 because 5 is in the tens place, and you round up to 700.

Example: 848 is 800 because 4 is in the tens place so you round down.

1) **753** _____   2) **215** _____   3) **101** _____

4) **718** _____   5) **944** _____   6) **494** _____

7) **126** _____   8) **820** _____   9) **925** _____

10) **733** _____   11) **576** _____   12) **613** _____

13) **776** _____   14) **908** _____   15) **490** _____

16) **639** _____   17) **156** _____   18) **399** _____

19) **787** _____   20) **895** _____

Worksheet 2

Addition

Instructions: In the ones columns add down, in the tens columns add down, and in the hundreds columns add down.

1) 400
   + 394
   ‾‾‾‾‾

2) 222
   + 161
   ‾‾‾‾‾

3) 525
   + 474
   ‾‾‾‾‾

4) 372
   + 620
   ‾‾‾‾‾

5) 502
   + 424
   ‾‾‾‾‾

6) 505
   + 434
   ‾‾‾‾‾

7) 450
   + 547
   ‾‾‾‾‾

8) 420
   + 523
   ‾‾‾‾‾

9) 131
   + 860
   ‾‾‾‾‾

10) 426
    + 503
    ‾‾‾‾‾

11) 448
    + 151
    ‾‾‾‾‾

12) 415
    + 464
    ‾‾‾‾‾

13) 222
    + 461
    ‾‾‾‾‾

14) 602
    + 354
    ‾‾‾‾‾

15)   505
  + 434
  ‾‾‾‾‾

16)   450
  + 547
  ‾‾‾‾‾

17)   220
  + 533
  ‾‾‾‾‾

18)   531
  + 420
  ‾‾‾‾‾

19)   486
  + 203
  ‾‾‾‾‾

20)   200
  + 574

Worksheet 3

Missing Place Value

Instructions: Look at the sum, find the digit that is missing, and add the place value it holds.

Example: $6 + 40 + \_\_\_ = 746$; There is a place for ones, tens, and the missing value is in the hundreds place. Therefore, 700 goes in the blank.

1) $5 + 30 + \_\_\_\_ = 735$ 2) $9 + 40 + \_\_\_\_ = 849$

3) $9 + \_\_\_\_ + 100 = 199$ 4) $\_\_\_\_ + 20 + 800 = 826$

5) $\_\_\_\_ + 60 + 500 = 564$ 6) $4 + 60 + \_\_\_\_ = 664$

7) $\_\_\_\_ + 20 + 700 = 720$ 8) $4 + 10 + \_\_\_\_ = 114$

9) $5 + \underline{\quad} + 200 = 265$

10) $\underline{\quad} + 80 + 200 = 285$

11) $2 + 70 + \underline{\quad} = 672$

12) $4 + 20 + \underline{\quad} = 824$

13) $6 + \underline{\quad} + 700 = 766$

14) $1 + \underline{\quad} + 600 = 661$

15) $4 + 20 + \underline{\quad} = 524$

16) $1 + 70 + \underline{\quad} = 971$

17) $5 + \underline{\quad} + 300 = 365$

18) $1 + \underline{\quad} + 400 = 451$

19) $4 + 40 + \underline{\quad} = 544$

20) $7 + 70 + \underline{\quad} = 777$

Worksheet 4

Telling Time

Instructions: Write the correct time on the spaces under each clock.

Where the short hand is located tells the hour, and the big hand tells

the minutes.

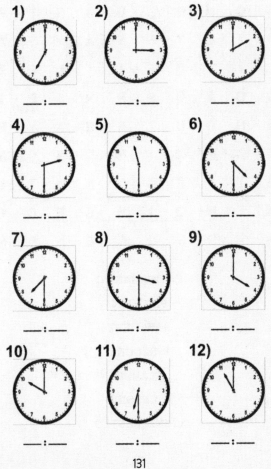

1) ___ : ___

2) ___ : ___

3) ___ : ___

4) ___ : ___

5) ___ : ___

6) ___ : ___

7) ___ : ___

8) ___ : ___

9) ___ : ___

10) ___ : ___

11) ___ : ___

12) ___ : ___

Chapter 1 Solution

ENTHUSIASTIC

FRICTION

IMPATIENT

INSECURE

PLAGUE

RECESSION

UNINTERESTED

Chapter 2 Solution

CONSCIOUS

PREDICTED

PULPIT

SACRIFICE

SUBDIVISION

TENSION

VOLUNTEER

Chapter 3 Solution

DREARY

HYPOTHESIS

INTENTIONAL

MISCHIEF

ORGANISMS

PARANOID

RESOLUTIONS

Chapter 4 Solution

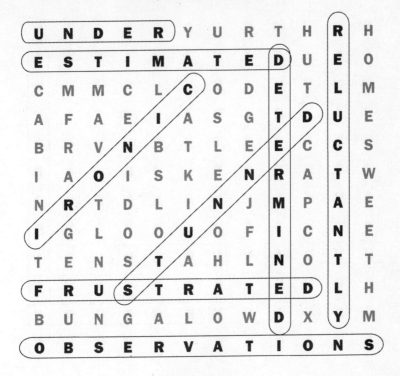

DETERMINED

FRUSTRATED

IRONIC

OBSERVATIONS

RELUCTANTLY

STUNNED

UNDERESTIMATED

Chapter 5 Solution

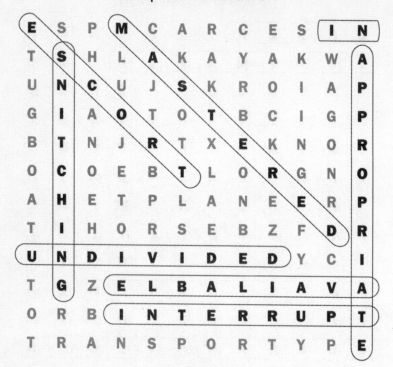

AVAILABLE

ESCORT

INAPPROPRIATE

(hint: find "appropriate" and connect "in")

INTERRUPT

MASTERED

SNITCHING

UNDIVIDED

Chapter 6 Solution

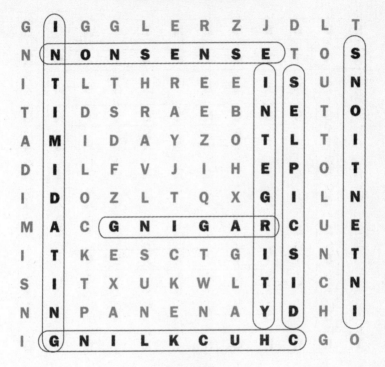

CHUCKLING

DISCIPLES

INTEGRITY

INTENTIONS

INTIMIDATING

NONSENSE

RAGING

Chapter 7 Solution

```
S  D  E  S  S  E  N  T  I  W  D  O
A  N  T  I  C  I  P  A  T  I  O  N
S  E  A  R  C  H  I  N  G  C  W  X
F  S  C  O  U  N  S  E  L  I  N  G
O  T  S  P  E  A  K  A  U  P  S  R
R  R  C  F  E  A  R  N  O  T  I  E
W  E  N  H  E  I  S  N  O  W  Z  S
O  S  E  I  T  D  A  R  C  Y  E  O
R  S  T  Y  T  I  R  A  L  C  F  L
D  E  N  I  N  T  H  G  I  E  N  V
S  D  I  S  F  U  N  S  E  V  E  E
T  E  R  R  O  R  I  Z  I  N  G  D
```

ANTICIPATION

CLARITY

COUNSELING

DOWNSIZE

STRESSED

TERRORIZING

WITNESSED

Answer Keys

**Rounding
Worksheet 1**

1) 800
2) 200
3) 100
4) 700
5) 900
6) 500
7) 100
8) 800
9) 900
10) 700
11) 600
12) 600
13) 800
14) 900
15) 500
16) 600
17) 200
18) 400
19) 800
20) 900

**Addition
Worksheet 2**

1) 794
2) 383
3) 999
4) 992
5) 926
6) 939
7) 997
8) 943
9) 991
10) 929
11) 599
12) 879
13) 683
14) 956
15) 939
16) 997
17) 753
18) 951
19) 689
20) 774

**Missing Place Values
Worksheet 3**

1) 700
2) 800
3) 90
4) 6
5) 4
6) 600
7) 0
8) 100
9) 60
10) 5
11) 600
12) 800
13) 60
14) 60
15) 500
16) 900
17) 60
18) 50
19) 500
20) 700

**Telling Time
Worksheet 4**

1) 7:00
2) 3:00
3) 2:00
4) 2:30
5) 11:30
6) 4:30
7) 7:30
8) 3:30
9) 4:00
10) 10:00
11) 6:30
12) 11:00

Credit to: http://www.homeschoolmath.net/worksheets/grade_2.php

Acknowledgments

Last weekend I had a reunion in Virginia with the girls I grew up with. It was so much fun thinking back on old times. Remembering all the times we got into it and all the stuff that made us mad at each other way back then seemed so small now. And when we talked about why we all acted out or why we even had issues, there was always something bigger going on that got us off track.

Thankfully, even when we were in elementary school we gave each other grace and spoke up when someone was trippin'. True friends tell each other the truth. And that truth is always said in love.

You see, the Word teaches us to treat each other as we'd want to be treated. I'm sure you don't want to be bulled, yelled at, talked about, or mistreated. So don't do that to anyone else. And if you have problems with your buddies—tell them. Choose to be the best person you can be. Friendships aren't easy; nor is life. But good friends can help you through anything. So embrace the blessings of having close friends and cherish them with your words and actions.

I am blessed as I think of all the folks that lend a hand to me writing cool novels.

For my parents, Dr. Franklin and Shirley Perry, I want to say thank you for raising me in a loving home and teaching me how to appropriately speak what's on my mind.

For my Moody/Lift Every Voice team, especially, Karen Waddles, I want to say thanks for going to bat for me, for your work, and for getting behind me.

For my precious extended family, Ciara Roundtree, Dennis Perry, Leslie Perry, and Franklin Perry. I want to say your love makes me strong.

For my friends who gave input into this series, Sarah Lundy, Jenell Clark, Vanessa Davis Griggs, Carol Hardy, Lois Barney, Veronica Evans, Sophia Nelson, Laurie Weaver, Taiwanna Brown-Bolds, Lakeba Williams, Jackie Dixon, Vickie Davis, Kim Monroe, Jan Hatchett, Veida Evans, and Deborah Bradley. I want to say thank you so much for truly telling me your thoughts on the title.

For my children, Dustyn Leon, Sydni Derek, and Sheldyn Ashli, I want to say you all mean so much to me, and I love being your mom.

For my husband, Derrick Moore, I want to say thank you for bearing with me as I labor to make my writing career work.

For my new young readers, I want to say that I pray this book will inspire you to always stand for what is right.

And to my Savior, Jesus Christ, I want to say thank You for giving me a powerful purpose—to pen titles that point people to You.

Lift every voice and sing
Till earth and heaven ring,
Ring with the harmonies of Liberty;
Let our rejoicing rise
High as the listening skies,
Let it resound loud as the rolling sea.
Sing a song full of the faith that the dark past has taught us,
Sing a song full of the hope that the present has brought us,
Facing the rising sun of our new day begun
Let us march on till victory is won.

The Black National Anthem, written by James Weldon Johnson in 1900, captures the essence of Lift Every Voice Books. Lift Every Voice Books is an imprint of Moody Publishers that celebrates a rich culture and great heritage of faith, based on the foundation of eternal truth—God's Word. We endeavor to restore the fabric of the African-American soul and reclaim the indomitable spirit that kept our forefathers true to God in spite of insurmountable odds.

We are Lift Every Voice Books—Christ-centered books and resources for restoring the African-American soul.

For more information on other books and products
written and produced from a biblical perspective, go to
www.lifteveryvoicebooks.com or write to:

Lift Every Voice Books
820 N. LaSalle Boulevard
Chicago, IL 60610
www.lifteveryvoicebooks.com